MAX'S CAMPERVAN CASE FILES BOOK 10

DEATH SLIDES AND Cheese Pies

TYLER RHODES

Copyright © 2025 Tyler Rhodes

All rights reserved. This book or any portion thereof may not be reproduced or used in any manner whatsoever without the express written permission of the author except for the use of brief quotations in a book review.

This is a work of fiction. Names, characters, businesses, places, events and incidents are either the products of the author's imagination or used in a fictitious manner. Any resemblance to actual persons, living or dead, or actual events is purely coincidental.

Dedicated to pie fans all over the world.

Chapter 1

I gulped, then stammered, "I'm not so sure this is a good idea," sweating not because of the May heat but because of the absolute, gut-wrenching terror of the sight before me. Okay, not before me, but below me.

"Of course it is." Min smiled merrily, her cheeks flushed with excitement, golden blond hair bouncing as she jigged excitedly from the top of the ridiculously high tower we'd just climbed. "It'll be fun. It's the highest in the country and brand new for the cheese pie festival, so what's the problem?" She tucked a long curl behind her ear, and such a lovely ear it was, along with the rest of her.

My ex-wife was brimming with energy, having slimmed down over the spring, and now keen as anything to show off her already tanned arms and legs. Blue eyes sparkled as she glanced at what awaited us, then drifted back to meet my own darting orbs.

"That's what I'm worried about. It's new, so how do we know it's safe? And how can it be? We must be fifty feet up. That isn't right."

"Fifty-seven feet actually."

"That doesn't make me feel better. Min, tell me again why we're doing this?" I gripped the handrail tightly and tried to focus on her rather than the wide red slide, known as a death slide, that dropped almost vertically from the tower perched atop a steep hill which made the whole thing even more dizzyingly terrifying in a way I had never experienced before. Min seemed immune, and was actually enjoying the height and the anticipation of what awaited us; I couldn't figure out why.

"Because it's fun! Can you believe how high we are?"

"Of course I can! I'm trying not to think about it. Are you sure it's safe?"

"Max, they wouldn't let us go on it if it wasn't. You just sit on the edge and drop off. I know it looks vertical, but it isn't. You'll slow once you hit the curvy bit, go whizzing along at only forty miles an hour, then launch off the end into the lake. It's incredible, and the kids that have already gone are splashing around having a great time."

"What if people drown? And what do you mean, only forty? It takes the campervan ten minutes to get up to that speed."

"You mean what if you drown, don't you?" she teased, nudging me in the ribs rather forcibly, her excitement beginning to bubble over. "Don't worry, they have stewards in the water to help, but you won't need it. You're a great swimmer."

"Not after launching off what amounts to a giant ski slope wearing shorts and a vest, I'm not. What about getting burns from the wood? That always used to happen to me as a kid on slides."

"That's why they give you the sack. Make sure to use yours. We have to go now, as people will be waiting. See, they're already coming up behind us."

I turned to Dave and his young assistant in panic and asked, "Dave, you said you built this thing, and you've not had any issues, right?"

"Of course not! It's solid as a rock. I ran the old slide for years, but this is different. Had the best crew building it, and all the tests have been done."

"It looks like it kept you fit," noted Min, eyeing the sixty-plus year old man up and down.

"Ay, well, I also run. That's my thing. Got one of those posh tracker watches so I can see my route and it has maps and everything. Back in the day, I used to be a paramedic. The things I saw made me get my act together and stay as fit as I can for as long as I can. I don't want to go out like some of those people did."

I glared at them both, Min grinning, Dave seemingly nonplussed by my reticence. Dave's strong, tanned, and veined forearms gripped the rail lightly, his cut-off sleeves, grubby jeans, and lined face making him look more like a boozer than a runner, and yet he seemed utterly relaxed and confident.

"Go on then," encouraged Min.

"You'll be fine, lad," said Dave, dragging lank, greying hair behind his large ears. "People are waiting now, so best take your turn."

We watched the snake of visitors slowly climbing the steps that crossed back and forth around the tower, everyone laughing and chatting excitedly as they ascended. I swallowed, and wondered if it was better to perform the walk of shame back down past them, or bite the bullet and trust I'd survive. Min had always loved fairground rides of all description, and was seemingly immune to fear when it came to heights. I preferred to keep my feet on solid ground and not tempt fate, but I'd agreed to this, and it was the first day together for ages, and I was the one who'd suggested we come here.

What I hadn't known when I invited her was that the cheese pie festival had this new, ridiculous attraction to draw in the crowds, and boy had it worked. I had a perfect bird's-eye view of the festival from our vantage point, and the place was packed. No time for that now, though, as the young lad tapping his foot beside me, apparently in charge of everyone's safety, was glaring and clearly about to send me back down unless I took the offered sack and went for it.

"Fine, but if I die it's your fault," I told Min. I spun to Dave and said, "Yours too. You built this, so it's on you."

"My brave man." She stood on tiptoe, her five foot five meaning I had to bend at the knee to receive the welcome gift, then she handed me the sack.

Trying to look brave, knowing I wasn't, I sat on the edge of the platform then slid inside the sack, legs dangling into nothing, and looked down. A wave of dizziness and nausea threatened to overwhelm me as I sweated badly and my heart hammered, but I clenched my jaw, turned to Min and smiled, and she nodded her encouragement.

"See you at the bottom," I gasped, gripping the edges tight.

For a moment, the world turned silent, then sound came rushing back in and I gasped with relief.

"Um, Max, are you going to let go?" asked Min, crouching beside me.

"Oh, er, right. I thought I had. I'm still here at the top, aren't I?"

"Maybe you should take the stairs? I don't want you to do anything that's scaring you so much. Come on, let's get you down." Min held out her hand and I reached out, then snatched my trembling hand away and shook my head.

"No, I'm doing this." With every ounce of my being protesting that this was a bad idea as why would you ever drop off such a height, I nevertheless released my grip and leaned forward. But it was too much, and I knew I was going to bottle it, so was beyond shocked when the kid in charge of my safety stepped forward.

"Enjoy the ride," he cheered, then shoved me in the back. I tried to grab the side rail but to no avail. I was falling into nothingness, sure my fate was sealed.

"Oi, you can't shove the punters," warned Dave, but it was too late.

As I plummeted, I had what can only be described as an end-of-life flashback. It was more of a shock than being shoved to my certain death by a spotty, bored teenager who nevertheless should have known better and would be losing his job in a few seconds when I went splat.

Rather than my entire life flashing before my eyes, it held four things and four things only. Min, Anxious, Mum, and Dad. That was it. Still images of them smiling, laughing, eating sausages greedily—that was Dad, not Anxious—tails wagging, heads cocked, curls bouncing, high heels reflecting the sun in a field, polka dot dresses, all wrapped up in the love felt for them and the love I knew they had for me.

I'd expected life experiences, maybe even lessons learned, but no, it was more than that. I relinquished myself to the inevitable, accepting of my fate, lamenting Min and I weren't married again, but it was all good, and I acknowledged that life had been interesting, great, in fact. I had nothing to complain about.

Which is why it came as a surprise when I bumped onto the hard wood of the death slide. My eyes sprang open of their own accord, the traitors, as no way would I do it voluntarily, and I screamed as the true extent of the rest of my journey was laid out before me. At least I was actually making contact with the slide's surface now, but it was ridiculously steep and there was a very long way to go. Down I slid, hurtling towards my doom, faster and faster as the polished wood whizzed by. I got friction burns along the sides of my legs but hardly felt a thing, and as I lay back I went faster, the thick hessian sack making my descent smooth and, I was shocked to discover, rather enjoyable in a terrifying, where's the toilet kid of way.

What a rush! The slide arced gracefully, but I didn't slow as my momentum carried me past the worst of the near vertical and onto an angle I could handle. I felt weightless, and awesome! Maybe Min was right and this was fun.

Then I glanced forward and noted the lake far, far below, and the people splashing in the water, the crowds on the shore, the stalls, the vehicles, the campervan field, and was that Vee, sparkling in the sunlight, my 67 beauty recognisable because she was the best of the lot, although I was slightly biased.

No way would I survive this.

"Goodbye, Vee. We had some great times," I said as a prayer. "You were the best. Cramped, slow, sometimes stinky, but I wouldn't change a thing."

As I approached the end of the slide, I squeezed my eyes shut and let the silence envelop me. I launched into the air and awaited whatever was on the other side in the big wild campsite in the sky, and hoped I'd get a good spot and could use my camping chair. Then I landed with a whack, bounced on my bum, sailed skyward, then somersaulted and landed face first in the lake.

I spluttered to the surface, erupted from the water, and gasped, shocked to be alive, grateful for it. A young man stood up to his waist with his hands out and helped me to stand, then asked, "All good? What a rush, eh?" face alight with merriment.

"All good, thanks."

"Wanna go a second time? Most do. If you head over there," he pointed to the shallows, "you can nip up the steps and enjoy it all over again."

"Um, I think I'll pass. Can I wait for my friend? She's coming down next."

"Sure, just stand back. Health and safety and all that." He indicated behind him, so after handing him the soggy sack I waded through the surprisingly warm water, the children splashing around me happily, then turned and shielded my eyes from the grinning sun, declaring all was well in the world and the sky would remain clear and blue the whole glorious day long.

I felt reborn, like a new man, or an old one who'd defied the gods and somehow managed to survive the awful trial I'd just participated in, and let out a whoop for joy. I did it! I went down the death slide and lived to tell the tale.

Min stood atop the astonishingly high tower, the true extent of it from my vantage point almost beyond comprehension. Perched on the hill, it was like being at the bottom of a man made mountain, a sea of red wood dropping to a long slide then the lake, but I just couldn't see the sense of it. Surely it was an accident waiting to happen? With me here, that was a given, as it had been weeks since I'd been embroiled in a murder mystery. Now here I was, right where one was sure to occur.

"I must have been mad to invite Min to this. What was I thinking?" I grumbled. "Not that I knew the slide would be this big."

I'd heard about the cheese pie festival from a fellow vanlifer a few weeks back and had invited Min who was rather too keen to come, and now I knew why. But for her I'd do anything, although I doubted I would have gone through with the slide unless that idiot had shoved me. Still, it meant we had a few days together staying at the festival, as it ran from this Friday to the Sunday morning and then people were allowed to stay until the Monday but the festival would be closed and the cleanup begun.

The site was stunning, set in the grounds of a stately home, although the house was gone, just the small cottages left after it had fallen into ruin over the decades until rescued by a charity that did what it could to bring in income. The cheese pie festival was one of the highlights of the year, attracting people from far and wide, most notably as it combined it with a campervan meet-up, and for a very agreeable price, so here I was, and alive to enjoy it.

The love of my life saluted, then sat and swung herself from safety onto the perilous drop, her cry of joy ringing out around the lake, and I marvelled at her bravery. She was actually enjoying herself. I shook my head in disbelief, then dragged back my soaking long brown locks from my face, and stroked my beard, bushy again after a tidy up a month ago.

Min shot down the death slide, and all the while I couldn't shake the feeling of impending doom. This was a terrible idea. Why were we putting ourselves in harm's way like this? Not us personally, but being somewhere so dangerous meant surely something bad would happen and someone with a grudge was sure to use the slide as a means of committing murder. Maybe that was why we were here?

Withdrawal from the excitement and thrill of solving a crime, working out the clues, and knowing we'd helped?

I dragged my eyes from Min and surveyed the lake, sure a corpse would float by at any moment, but all it contained was over-excited children and just as happy adults. The water was warm, the air the same, and the only risk seemed to be the lack of sunscreen—there would be some serious cases of sunburn this evening.

An almighty whoop caused me to spin sharply and witness Min launch from the end of the slide, sail through the air, then spin before diving headfirst into the water and emerging right in front of me, like a dolphin arcing gracefully from the ocean.

I caught her in my arms as she glided towards me, and before I had the chance to control myself I kissed her on the lips and pulled her in tight, her warm, glistening skin sending a shiver of delight through me. Min clung to my shoulders and sighed, then trembled, and I knew I'd done the right thing.

"Sorry, got caught up in the moment." I smiled sheepishly.

"So did I!" The woman I adored the most in the whole world wrapped her arms tight around me and looked into my eyes. "What a perfect day." She kissed me in return, slow and lingering, then we broke apart and laughed, the adrenaline surely the reason for such a display of affection. "Gosh, don't know where that came from. How awesome was that? Want to have another go?"

"Absolutely not. I want to sit on the grass, dry off, and try to calm my nerves. You go if you want to, but I'm never leaving the ground again."

"Spoilsport." Min reached out and teased a wayward strand of my hair behind my ear then nodded her approval. "Handsome as always. Look at you all hunky and glistening in the sunshine. Your muscles are bigger than ever."

"I've been using the gym membership three or four times a week and it's been great. Plus, I get to have a sauna and a proper shower too."

"It shows. Come on, let's go and get Anxious. He'll be having a meltdown being left alone for so long."

"I'll be there in a moment. Just need to catch my breath." Min leaned close, her breath warm, the scent of her shampoo strong, but I refrained from taking a sniff as for some reason she found it weird. She looked deep into my eyes, but said nothing, then smiled. "You can read my mind, can't you?" I gulped, grinning.

"Let me get out and see if I was right." She winked, then released me and waded to shore.

Watching her go, I knew she had read my thoughts, as she wiggled her bum suggestively, her very short cut-offs showing her fine shape, then she glanced coyly over her shoulder, shook out her hair, and pointed at me. "Gotcha!"

"Yes, I admit it," I shouted, "you are a beautiful woman, Min Effort, and I love you!"

The lake fell silent and all eyes turned to me. I felt the heat rise, but then laughed and admitted to anyone who was listening, "She's my ex-wife and I love her. She's a beautiful woman."

"Good on ya, mate," said a man beside me and slapped me on the back.

It was to a round of applause that I left the lake, and I didn't care.

Min was already sunning herself on our picnic blanket at the water's edge when I arrived, with Anxious cuddled up in her lap. He barked a welcome, then shook his head.

"You try going down that death slide then see if you find it so funny," I admonished.

My best buddy whined, glanced at the slide, shuddered, then curled up again, happy to be with Min, us a family again for a short while.

"This is perfect." Min sighed, then lay on her back and closed her eyes. "And nobody died."

"I know. Amazing, isn't it? Seems like this will just be a great holiday with lots of food, some cool vans to check out, and the weather is incredible. This will be awesome."

We lay there, side by side, hands clasped together, and let the world pass us by. Anxious snored, children played, adults chatted, and terrified fools screamed as they slid down the death slide.

After what felt like hours, I was surprised to find it was only half eleven, so sat up and asked, "Anyone fancy a walk? The stalls should be set up by now, and I'd like to see what vans have arrived. Let's stretch our legs then get lunch.

Anxious was up in a shot, only narrowly beating Min. Our stomachs rumbled as we caught the first whiff of the delicious offerings. Let the cheese pie festival begin!

Chapter 2

We'd arrived on Thursday afternoon after I picked Min up from the station. She hadn't fancied the drive and liked the relaxed trip by rail rather than stressing about directions. The site, a series of large fields leading down from where the old house had once stood, was sloped before levelling out around the lake, and it was here that most visitors and businesses were set up.

By the evening, the campervan field was close to capacity, but this wasn't exactly an event in the tens of thousands, more like a few thousand tickets plus those coming for the day, so we had plenty of room for the gazebo without encroaching on our neighbours. Especially as we managed to nab one of the many little hideaways tucked away around the trees down seemingly endless small tracks you'd never know were there unless you investigated.

It meant that although there were literally hundreds of vans and motorhomes by nightfall, it felt like we were alone. We'd relaxed, drunk wine, had a fire in a small foldable fire pit I'd splashed out on, and chilled our way through to bedtime before snuggling up on the rock n roll bed together, with Anxious taking more space than us as usual.

Friday morning brought glorious sunshine, an astonishing number of early arrivals, plus the traders were hurrying to set up their stalls, the focus on food, the cheese pies of all description the stars of the show.

It was a weird event, a Cheshire tradition I'd never heard of that had evolved over the years from people rolling pies down the hill to the peculiar attraction it had now become. From its formative years, the cheese pie fest had morphed into a celebration of all things food, but the giant pies followed on Saturday by the infamous pie rolling competition were the real draw. I was astonished to discover it brought people from all over the country.

Years back, some intrepid soul had built a long wooden slide that ran down the hill, and the winner was whoever managed to roll their pie the furthest across the lake. That slowly changed into a death slide being built, but it had seen better days and this year the charity had upped their game and built the monster I'd just had the misfortune of tumbling down. It meant not only would the competition be much more dramatic, but the death slide could be a nice earner as ticket sales for the event were at a record high this year.

We made our way slowly around the lake, smiling at the gathering crowds of families and pie aficionados, the van obsessives, and the understandably confused or bemused, a spring in our step and joy in our hearts. The day planned to be an awesome mix of sun, food, and great company. We headed back to Vee with our wet towels, pausing to chat with the other vanlifers or occasional users, many hanging out around their vans to show off their conversions or get inspired, and it did feel very special.

I'd avoided going to most of the campervan festivals, as although I was undoubtedly a true vanlifer now myself, it had still been less than a year since I took the plunge and became a nomad so I'd felt like an imposter, not worthy of the name. Many true vanlifers had been living out of their vehicles for years, even decades, but the more time I'd spent with others like me, the more I came to realise that it was only in the past few years that the movement had truly taken off.

It meant I was relaxed and keen to chat with those we met, Min too, swapping tips and getting inspired by fancy layouts, although I was still convinced that the layout

I'd inherited was better than many we encountered. The obsession with fancy hobs and sinks and water containers taking up valuable space inside vans was still in evidence, but it was those who'd opted for awnings or gazebos for their cooking whenever possible who seemed happiest with their setup. Yes, I still had the original sink, hob, and water container housing underneath, but they were only used when the weather was awful. Now I was in two minds about keeping them at all, and instead had opted for a piece of board over the hob to increase counter space.

I drooled at the latest slide-out drawers or fold-up tables that stuck out of the sides of the newer conversions, outdoor cooking now firmly the way forward for most. Especially the weekenders who could pick their days and travel when the weather promised to be nice. It freed up masses of interior space and stopped the cooking smells and inevitable mess from contaminating the interior.

We made it back to Vee half an hour later, keen to relax and be in our own private space, so after I hung up the towels and we changed into dry clothes, Min looking resplendent in a tight pink vest and black denim cut-offs with matching pink flip-flops, me in the usual black vest, faded denim shorts, and Crocs, we sat back with a cuppa and soaked up the atmosphere and sunned ourselves while Anxious napped in the shade, for some reason reticent to sleep under Vee like he usually preferred.

"Life doesn't get better than this," sighed Min, sipping her coffee and stretching her legs out, her red painted toes digging into the grass.

"Sure doesn't. I'm glad you came. This will be a great few days, and we even have nice weather. Should be an awesome event."

"It really should. I can't believe how popular it is. Imagine what it will be like tomorrow."

"Isn't the big event then?"

"Yep. A load of pie obsessive rolling their pies off the death slide into the lake. What a thing!"

"I bet the place will be rammed. But today's busy, too, and it's only early. What's going on later?"

"Max, didn't you look? This was your idea."

"I didn't want to spoil the surprise. I think there's music tonight, but this afternoon there's something going on too."

Min grabbed her phone from her bag beside her and spent a few minutes checking things out, then explained, "It's a giant pie competition today. All the competitors for tomorrow have to bake their largest pie today and the winner goes first tomorrow. That way, everyone knows what they're up against."

"Be careful. These things can get out of hand."

Min laughed, and waved a hand dismissively. "I think I can handle a few pies."

"I mean it, Min. People at these types of events take it really seriously. It's their reputation on the line and the winners will do great business tomorrow after the competition. They'll be up to all sorts to try to win, and you can bet there will be plenty of arguments and maybe a few fights."

"You're serious? Over pies?"

"Like I said, those on these competition circuits take it super seriously. But don't worry," I turned and grinned at her, "I'll protect you."

"My hero!" she laughed, feigning a swoon. "Whatever would I do without you?"

"Get assaulted by pie maniacs?" I suggested, stifling a laugh.

Min glanced around, wary of being overheard as people were constantly walking past, then leaned in and whispered, "Watch what you say. We don't want to make them cross."

"I'll be on my best behaviour." I winked and had to stifle a whoop when she pecked me on the cheek.

"Max, I, um… No, it doesn't matter." Min toyed with her hair and gnawed at her lip, a sure sign she was unsettled and clearly had something to say.

"What is it? Something wrong?"

"It's nothing. Just that, no, it can wait."

"Is it about us?" My heart beat fast, I got a sweat on, and began to grin uncontrollably. There was no doubt we'd been getting along better than ever, and the warmer weather seemed to have brought with it a heightened sense of anticipation. I knew it wasn't just me. Min felt it too. Summer was fast-approaching, and then it would be make or break time for our future. Would we have passed the test, proved our love, that we had a permanent, forever-together future before us, or realise we'd be better off apart? I knew what I wanted, and thought she felt the same, but as I'd learned, there were no guarantees in life.

"Yes, but it's silly. Let's leave it. I almost broke my own rule and began discussing our relationship again. Another time. Gosh, it's getting hot."

"Whatever you want. Maybe a cold drink rather than coffee? We could have wine. That would be nice."

"Max, it's just gone twelve. We've got all day and evening yet. Maybe a soft drink though?"

"Sure. And Anxious needs to cool down too. Look at him. He's panting."

We turned to the little guy curled up next to the coolbox under the collapsible table in the kitchen area of the gazebo, and he must have heard his name mentioned because he opened an eye and grinned.

"Feeling hot, buddy?" asked Min. "Let me get you a drink." Min emptied the small collapsible water bowl then topped it up with fresh from one of the bottles lined up neatly under the table, and the little guy crawled out on his belly then lapped eagerly.

"Wow, he was thirsty. It's warm, but not that hot. He needs proper shade."

"Anxious, why don't you go under Vee?" suggested Min. "That's your favourite spot anyway." When Anxious merely sat and cocked his head, Min turned to me and frowned, shrugging her shoulders.

"He's holding out in case he misses the pies. Anxious, buddy, have a nap. We'll head off in half an hour. Min and I are going to have a sneaky glass of wine."

"I thought you said we'd wait?"

"You said to wait. I'm on holiday and plan to enjoy the vibe."

"Your life is one long holiday," pouted Min.

"You could quit work if you wanted to. You know there's enough money from the rental properties. They're doing good, and there's money in the bank. Min, is everything okay at work?"

"It's fine. Busy, and stressful, and not as much fun as it used to be, but I honestly don't know what I'd do if I didn't have a job."

"Travel around with us and drink wine at midday?" I suggested with a raised eyebrow and I hoped a lighthearted enough tone.

"Sounds tempting." Min turned her attention back to the panting ball of awesomeness and suggested again, "Take a nap under Vee. It's nice and cool."

Anxious glanced from her to me, then to Vee, and stood, seemingly still reluctant.

"I know how to get him to go under." I slid forward off my chair, then crawled over on all fours and told Min, "We can go together."

"Don't be so silly," she laughed, but nevertheless dropped down then we began crawling across the grass the few metres to the van.

Anxious, always up for fun and games, wagged happily then shoved between us, but as we approached Vee, the strange graffiti still present on the side, but having not been messed with for many months, he stopped and his hackles rose. He whined, and backed away, causing us to exchange a look, but when Min called him with words of encouragement he trotted forward cautiously.

We crawled right up to the van, then lay on our backs and began to get under, but Anxious barked loudly then retreated to the gazebo.

"What's got into him?" I wondered, catching the frown on Min's face only inches from mine.

She sniffed, her face wrinkled in disgust, and gasped, "What is that awful smell? It stinks under here."

I sniffed deeply and caught a familiar tang of iron and other much worse things, sticking to the back of my tongue like a coating I could never remove, then warned, "Do not look under the van, do not move suddenly, and make sure you get out quickly. Trust me, and don't ask questions."

"Max, what are you talking about?"

I knew I shouldn't have, but I couldn't help myself, and I angled my head to inspect the underside of Vee. As I did, Anxious barked again then raced under Vee, nudged Min so she fell sideways, and as I reached out to her my arm caught on something much softer than any van's underside should be and a huge lump fell between us, pinning my arm.

Anxious went nuts barking and running back and forth between me, Min, and the corpse. Min screamed, I tried to hold down my breakfast, and with a yank I freed my arm, slid out backwards, and dragged her by the ankles as she scrabbled at the grass.

Once she was free, I lay on my belly and got my first proper look at what had stopped Anxious from taking up his favourite spot and gasped. The mangled body of a man somewhere between thirty and forty lay on his back, facing us, neck in a strange position, an arm bent in all the wrong places. His denim jeans, thick biker boots, and tank top over a check shirt were torn and bloodied, and the ground surrounding him was wet with what was clearly blood.

Min squeezed beside me and made a strange nervous clicking with her tongue, then grabbed hold of my arm for comfort. "Max, he's dead. How did he get here? Was he holding on to the underside? Is that possible?"

"I don't know. It's very low, and we only just fit, but he was wedged in there until we disturbed him. He's clearly dead, but I'll have to check." I reached out for his neck, but Min held tight and pulled my arm back.

"No, don't! He's covered in blood, and of course he's dead."

"Min, I have to be sure. He might need help." She released me, so I did my best to find a pulse then resorted to prising his eyelid open and checking his breath. With no indication he was still alive, I slid out with Min, then knew what I had to do so reached back under and carefully dragged the body out from under my beloved sixties campervan.

We stared down at the poor man, clearly deceased, and I noted the oil stains, the cuts and scrapes, his raw knuckles, and wondered what his back was like. His boots were almost worn through at the heels and toes, but I dared not turn him over to inspect the rest, as this was now obviously a crime scene.

"I'll go and get help," said Min, then flung herself at me and held me tight for a moment before moving back and smiling weakly. "There's an ambulance stationed near the entrance, with paramedics on standby by the lake too. Which one should I go to?"

"Whoever is nearest. There's also police by the food stalls, and security. Maybe the police would be best first. Let's all go."

I called for Anxious who was only too pleased to get away, so we hurried from the scene, past several cheery people outside their vans relaxing in the sun, then away towards the line of food stalls set back at the edge of the woods bordering the lake where the concentration of visitors would be the highest and everyone got a good view of the water and death slide.

Anxious led the way, with us right behind him. We tore past the last van, sped across open ground, then came to the first food stall, a cheese pie one, same as all the others, with the prime spot. As we passed marquee or table after table someone up ahead screamed. We exchanged a worried look then sped up as Anxious began to yip just around the bend, then skidded to a halt beside him and looked where he was focused.

A woman in her thirties with a dark ponytail and a white apron over a green shirt was red-faced and screaming as a crowd gathered and people came rushing over. Face down in a huge pie taking up the entire table was the head of a man.

"I think he's dead," she sobbed, then gently pulled his head from the pie.

Steam rose and everyone gasped as he was freed from the cheese and potato, his face bright red from the heat. His short, greying beard was covered in the filling, his wavy blond hair matted with bits of pastry, but it was the way his tongue stuck out as if to get a final taste of his creation that made everyone gag and me frown in confusion. Why on earth was his tongue out like that?

"Timmy!" yelled a woman as she rushed from behind the marquee with an armful of regular-sized pies then dropped the box as she caught sight of him lolling back in his chair, pie filling oozing down his chin.

"Tina, I'm so sorry, but Tim's dead," said the woman who had moved him.

"My husband! No, it can't be."

Tim's wife grabbed his shoulders and shook him, but he was clearly already gone. With a wail, she gave up and his head slumped forward. With an awful splat, he face-planted into the pie again, splattering everyone close with molten cheese and potato.

"Must have been a heart attack," someone commented from behind me.

"Or the heat," suggested someone else. "Heatstroke maybe."

Everyone began to offer an opinion while those who clearly knew the owners of the stall helped Tina and the other woman into chairs while they checked on Tim to ensure he really was dead.

Min and I looked at one another, wide-eyed and incredulous.

"This can't be a coincidence, can it?" she asked.

"Stranger things have happened," I said, the only reply that came to mind.

"Really?" Min's eyebrow threatened to pop off the top of her head as she glanced back to poor Tim, then towards Vee.

"Some weird stuff has happened over the last year, but no, this is by far the oddest. Come on, let's get the police."

Chapter 3

As people rushed towards us to see what was happening, Min and I gripped each other tightly and forced our way through the throng until we reached the end of the marquees and the police car and gazebo set up for the bored-looking officers on duty, just now easing from their chairs and glancing our way, wondering what the fuss was about.

"Officers, there's been a terrible accident," gasped Min. "Um, maybe not an accident, we don't know, but there's another problem at our van too. Quick! Hurry up." Min glanced at me and I squeezed her hand and smiled reassuringly, but she was shaken up and close to tears.

"Ma'am, please calm down and tell us what happened," soothed the young officer who must have been new to the job as he looked about twelve. His partner joined him, a young woman of similar age, both looking almost comical in their crisp uniforms, their fresh faces brightening at the hint of some action on what must have otherwise been a very ordinary day for them.

"What is it? Do you require assistance?" asked the woman.

"One of the stallholders, someone involved in the competition, is dead," I explained. "He's face down in a large pie."

"Heart attack?" asked the man.

"No idea. But that's not all, and the mangled corpse is a whole other story."

"Corpse!?" gasped the woman, already reaching for a radio at her breast. "What corpse?"

"He was under our van," said Min, regaining her composure. "Must have been trapped there. He's cut and mangled and his neck's at a funny angle. He's... he's..."

"Are you sure he's dead?" asked the man.

"He's dead," I grunted. "Can you get the paramedics? They need to check. And I suppose you better secure the scene."

"Thank you, sir, but I think we know how to handle a crime scene. If this is a crime scene," said the woman, bristling at my words. "Are you seriously telling us there are two bodies and this just happened?"

"We don't know how long the man under our van has been dead, but the other guy died a minute or two ago."

The officers exchanged a look, nodded to each other, then the woman called it in before using her mobile to alert the paramedics just around the lake a little where their ambulance was parked. They told us to lead the way, so we turned and hurried back the way we'd just come, everything happening so quickly we didn't have the chance to think about much beyond getting past the crowd of people gathered around the stall.

As is often the case when the authorities arrive, the crowd seemed to have a sixth sense and parted to give the officers access; we followed in their wake. The dead man, Tim, was still in the chair, his face smeared with pie filling. His wife, Tina, and the distraught assistant who had screamed when she found him were each holding a cloth as they tried unsuccessfully to clean Tim's face properly.

People were talking loudly, some rather insensitive about what could have happened, many still offering opinions on heatstroke and heart attacks, whilst others merely gawped at the sight of the man and the large, ruined pie on the table. The stall itself was piled high with all manner of various pies, from huge like the one that had done for Tim to more regular sizes that were clearly the main earner for High Pies, the name on the sign. There was nothing unusual about the stall or the marquee behind where several vehicles were parked, as the entire row was set up in a similar manner, each with a marquee with the sides down to hide their prized pie for the competition later on this afternoon.

The police asked everyone to disperse, the young officers flustered and close to panicking. I guessed this was one of their first jobs and was surprised they didn't have an experienced officer with them, then recalled that up the hill a police van was stationed most likely with the older officers taking it easy and letting the youngsters cover what should have been a non-event in terms of criminal activity.

People wandered off as there was nothing to be done, the crowd thinning as the officers called out once again for everyone to go about their business. Min and I held back and watched proceedings, unsure what to do, but as the minutes ticked by and the paramedics and more officers finally arrived, we knew we couldn't hang around here any longer. We had our own body to deal with, and although I felt for Tina and her deceased husband, the corpse at our pitch was much more concerning.

I tried to grab an officer and instil some urgency in them but they were distracted by the problem of moving Tim and doing so without causing more upset for his wife or the assistant, all whilst dozens of people remained rooted to the spot, watching. In the end, I had to actually stand in front of the young man who we'd reported this to and insist they come and take a look.

"Sorry, got totally sidetracked. We'll be there in a moment, I promise. Can you return to your vehicle, sir, and ensure nothing is disturbed?"

"Yes, okay, but hurry. The guy is in a right state, and although I feel sorry for Tim, murder is surely more pressing?"

"Murder?" His eyes rose, a dubious smile on his clear complexion, and he chuckled. "Let's not get carried away. People die, you know? Most likely an unfortunate accident."

"He was under our van! He's cut up badly. Maybe it was an accident, but maybe not. I, er, have a habit of getting embroiled in murder mysteries. Just hurry, please."

With a shake of his head, and a wry smile, clearly thinking I was being overly dramatic, he turned from me and pulled an older officer to one side and spoke to him while they both glanced at me and Min repeatedly.

We backed out from the press of bodies and slowly, and very reluctantly, returned to Vee with Anxious keeping close, mindful of the fact he was small and people were liable to step on him if he wasn't careful.

It was a real relief to escape the chaos, but we were both dazed and feeling out of it as we passed from the scene of the death into the sunshine on the track by the lake then headed to Vee. Neither of us spoke, merely held on to each other and put one foot in front of the other numbly. Yet again, what was meant to be a peaceful camping trip had turned into something much more sinister. And yet, beneath the sadness and the sympathy of the families, I felt that familiar tingle of excitement and anticipation at being involved in another mystery.

But was it a murder? Two deaths were a mighty coincidence, but Tim's death truly did appear to be an unfortunate heart attack or something similar, while the body under our van was much more perplexing. We kept our heads down as we passed the other vans, not in the mood for chatting, the excited bathers and children running around happily already disconcerting enough as it was so at odds with what had happened.

Anxious refused to go past the entrance to the gazebo that was butted up tight against the van, so we left him there and approached the corpse cautiously.

"Who do you think he is?" asked Min, brushing at her hair irritably. "Think he has anything to do with Tim?"

"I can't see how, but it's possible. What I'd like to know is what was he doing under the van? Min, did we drag this poor guy all over the place? I don't remember hitting anything, and Vee drove fine, so how was he stuck under her all this time?"

"Maybe he was lying in the road somewhere close, like when we arrived here, and we drove over him and snagged him somehow. Remember, there were speed bumps at the entrance and along the lane for a while so traffic slows on the site, so maybe we mistook him for a speed bump." Min gnawed at her lip, tears welling.

"For his sake, I hope so. I'd hate to think he was alive under there while we drove here. Min, I'm so sorry. This isn't going to be the relaxing trip we anticipated. Two deaths, and it isn't even lunchtime yet." Despite the circumstances, my stomach rumbled, and as if to tease us the strong smell of baking pies drifted on the gentle breeze, ruffling our hair, the promise of a beautiful summer and long, lazy days almost overpowering.

"Hey, it isn't your fault, and I'm sure there's an explanation. Maybe for once it is just an accident."

"Is that what you really think?" I stared into the concerned eyes of the woman I loved more than anything and saw the truth of it. "You don't think this was an accident, do you?"

"Not really, no. Do you?"

"I'd love it if it was, but you know how these things usually go. I think the best thing to do is take a proper look at him and see if we can come up with something before the police arrive. They will be here in a minute, I'm sure, so let's do this now. Are you up to it? I know it's horrible, but this is my home, maybe our home, and the thought of him being under Vee and bits of him stuck there, it's just…"

"Hey, it's okay. I understand. And although I don't live in Vee full time, I do think of her as our home. Come on, let's go take a look at the body." Min squeezed my arm, pecked me on the cheek, then took my hand. Together, we walked through the gazebo then stood over the ravaged man and tried to take in the sight without urging.

"Oh, Max, it's worse than I remembered. What on earth happened here? His clothes are ruined, and he's covered in oil, and his boots are almost worn through. He must have been dragged and that wore out the heels, but how did he stay put under there? And why? Think he might be an illegal immigrant or something?"

"That's unlikely. I haven't been anywhere near a port or somewhere he might have come ashore, and why would you choose a VW campervan to hitch a ride on like this? Maybe he wanted to sneak into the pie festival as he couldn't afford it. Yes, that must be it!" I smiled and nodded, as the more I thought about it, the more that made sense.

"You're right! Why didn't I think of that? Yes, he most likely rolled under when we stopped before we paid to get in, grabbed hold, then regretted it when we went over the speed bumps. I bet he got caught with his clothes and couldn't get free, and then he got mangled. We only just scraped over the speed bumps and we both heard the crunch on the last one. That must have been this guy. The poor thing."

"Let's take a closer look. Min, I know we shouldn't move him, but we've already done that, so let's take a look at his back. I'd like to have this figured out in my head before the police come so we can enjoy the rest of the festival. You want to help?"

"I don't want to, but I will. You're right, we need to solve this right away so we can relax. It's awful, but if it was an accident I want to be sure."

I hurried over to Anxious and stroked his back until he stopped shaking. When he lay down, I gave him a few biscuits which had the desired effect and he wagged happily, then with a smile from me tucked in. Back with Min, we nodded grimly then squatted beside the man and studied him intently. As before, there wasn't much to see. Faded, very ripped jeans, boots, red and black chequered shirt, grey tank top, short mousy hair somewhere between blond and brown, a slightly round face, but a well-muscled body with just a little extra weight.

He was clearly European, and could have been Polish or Welsh. He had that stocky build common to both countries, although I knew that was a stereotype. A thick silver curb chain was tight at his wrist, but there was no watch or other jewellery, no bag, but he might have had a phone in his back pocket, possibly a wallet too.

"Ready?" I asked.

"Ready."

We got onto our knees then gently rolled him over as best we could with his arm still at an unnatural angle until with a wincing crunch he folded over on it and flopped onto his stomach.

Min gasped, I closed my eyes for a second, and we both took several deep breaths before looking again.

It was not a pretty sight.

"You can leave this to me if you'd prefer?" I suggested, noting Min's colour had drained and she looked white as a sheet.

"I will. I'll make a coffee. We're going to need it." With a kiss and a squeeze of my arm, Min stepped over to Vee, taking a wide berth of the man, then stopped, clearly befuddled, before smiling sadly and hurrying back into the gazebo where the cooker and coffee stuff was.

With the comforting sounds of her clattering away in the background, I let it slowly fade until my attention was on the unfortunate bloke on the ground before me. It took all my willpower to look, but I owed it to him to at least try to figure out what had happened, even though I knew the police were better suited to reading the signs of accidents like this as it wasn't anything I'd encountered before.

In my albeit limited experience of such things, meaning none, the wounds and the way the clothes were worn away were what I'd expect if someone had been dragged along under the van. Most were on his back, his hamstrings and bottom, and the heels of his boots. They were an expensive brand, one I'd balked at buying for myself last winter, instead opting for a cheaper pair from an

Army and Navy store. The back of his head was matted with blood but not as damaged as I'd expected, but something had clearly happened to his neck and right arm —most likely the neck injury had killed him.

The faded outline of a phone was clearly visible in his left back pocket, but there was no phone there. He obviously kept it there all the time and wore the jeans almost daily for the fade to be so strong, and the whiskers at the back of the knee proved these were jeans the man wore almost constantly. Sticking out of the other pocket was a piece of paper barely visible, and I was shocked it had remained there as the pocket was badly damaged. I snapped a photo, then leaned forward and eased it out by the corner, mindful of fingerprints. High Pies, the card read in the same style as the banner at the pie stand, the flying pie logo above the typography. I snapped that, too, then replaced it just as I'd found it.

Rifling through his other pockets, I found nothing, and with his eyes staring at me accusingly, I carefully rolled him onto his back and crossed his arms then closed his eyes, hoping it gave him dignity in death, unsure whether I'd done the right thing or not.

"Max, are you okay?" Min squatted beside me, her gaze averted from the man, and smiled in sympathy.

"Um, I think so. Poor bloke. What a way to go. I think you might be right and the speed bumps did for him. He must have broken his neck and mangled his arm at the same time."

"At least it was just an accident. A terrible one, but this means we can enjoy the rest of our break. Sorry, is that really callous? I didn't mean it to be. I wanted to spend time with you both, and this is just so gruesome."

"Don't feel bad for wanting to enjoy yourself. It's what I wanted too. For once, it does look like it was a terrible accident. The only thing that makes me concerned is the card I found in his back pocket. See?" I held up my phone and zoomed in on the name.

Min gasped, then batted my arm with a rather vicious slap and scowled at me. "You idiot!"

"What was that for?" I whined, rubbing at the red mark on my tanned forearm.

"Now we'll have to spend our time asking everyone questions and getting involved in Tim's death. No way is this a coincidence."

"It might be." The words sounded lame even to my ears, and Min merely glared at me, then a slow smile spread across her face.

"Oh no you don't. I know that look." I backed away and slumped to the ground, my legs out in front of me. Taking it as an invitation, Anxious trotted over, glanced from me to Min then back again, then settled on my legs and curled up, seemingly over the shock of the corpse.

"What look?" Min tried to look innocent, but there was no fooling me.

"The look you get when you're excited about solving a murder."

"I was pleased when we thought it was an accident. Um, not pleased, you know what I mean. Ugh, I'm getting flustered. All I mean is that it will be good to help out, try to figure out what happened to this poor man. That's a good thing, isn't it?"

"I guess," I said warily, knowing what she really felt. Cautiously, I asked, "You're excited, aren't you?"

"Okay, I admit it! I am. Is that awful? Am I a terrible person? You usually get to solve a mystery without me, or I'm just here for a while, but this time I'm around from the start, like at Christmas, and I want to help. We owe it to this man. He was under our home."

I couldn't help smiling at her words, despite the sombre mood. Our home! That had a nice ring to it.

Chapter 4

"I feel the same," I admitted. "It's awful, but this happened to us for a reason, same as it always does. Of all the people here whose van he could have been under, it's ours. And we've dealt with this kind of thing before. After almost a year, I've reconciled myself to things like this happening to me, and to you. We should be honest and admit that the buzz of trying to figure out the mystery is something we if not enjoy, then at least get a sense of satisfaction from solving. That's not bad, it's just normal human behaviour."

"Exactly! And you're so good at unravelling mysteries, so we should try our best to figure this out. It'll be fun, in a serious way," she added, frowning. The whole situation, like always, was confusing as emotions became mixed.

"Min, I get it. It's a difficult thing to put into words. How we feel about these murder mysteries is so complicated that I wouldn't know where to begin. Like we've said before, it is exciting, and detectives feel the same way. They enjoy the work, but that doesn't mean they don't have sympathy for the deceased or the families involved, or even the killers. It's never black and white. There's always something else going on. The human condition. It's a messed up, crazy world, and we're doing our best, the same as everyone else."

"Well said!" Min leaned over and wrapped her arms around me. I took a cheeky sniff of her hair. The scent was faint after our dip in the lake, but it still smelled like home. Like love.

"Stop that, you weirdo," she giggled, her breath warm on my ear.

"Min, I think we have issues. There's a dead man a few feet away and we're messing about."

"We're awful!" Min tumbled back onto her bum and threw her arms up as she looked skyward. "Forgive me."

As the guilt and the knot of remorse in my stomach intensified, I couldn't help asking, "Who are you talking to?"

"I'm not sure. Just hedging my bets. We've been doing this for too long, Max. Are we losing our empathy? I do feel bad for this man, truly I do, and I can't even look at him, but I was just breathing into your ear and getting hot and bothered."

"Really?" I asked, my heart beating fast, pinpricks of sweat beading to the surface.

"Hey, that isn't helping."

"Min, it's alright. We're good people. These are natural reactions. In the sight of death, your brain often goes a little wacky. Plenty of people laugh at funerals, smile when they want to cry, and we're simply doing what we can to handle the situation. It's a coping mechanism. We both feel for this poor man, hate that he's dead, and want justice. We also need to figure out if the pie man, Tim, has anything to do with this."

Min scooted over, eyes gleaming, and asked, "Do you think the deaths are related? How can they be? It must be a coincidence. When do you think the man from under the van died?"

"He's still warm, so I reckon a few hours, if that. Hopefully, the police will be able to tell us more."

As was the way with these things, it was at this precise moment that a troop of police and paramedics arrived. Joining the two young officers were two much older men in uniform, large stomachs and sagging chins indicating they were not new to the force and most likely approaching retirement so got the easy jobs, along with two paramedics, a man and a woman, sweltering in their thick uniforms, each lugging a heavy bag and more equipment on their backs, no help from the police.

"What seems to be the issue, sir?" asked the larger of the two older officers, completely ignoring Min.

We stood, and Min gripped my hand tight, taking umbrage, and I felt the tension travel from her to me. This would not go well unless the cop suddenly got out of the stone-age in the next several seconds.

"We found a body under our van. We were coming to tell someone when the man, Tim, died in his pie."

"Yes, most unfortunate. Waste of a lovely pie." The corner of his mouth twitched as the other older officer laughed, but he got a nasty look from the young officers and the paramedics, who bustled forward, shouldering him out of the way without apology. There was clearly a history here, and not a nice one you'd write on a greeting card.

"Have some respect!" snapped the paramedic as she bent to the body and glared at him.

"Just trying to lighten the mood. Sir, I apologise if I caused offence. Now, you say you found him under your van? How did he get there? Did you run him over and he got caught?"

"We," and I emphasised the we, "assume so. We aren't sure. The only bumps we felt were the speed bumps at the entrance to the site, but we saw no body. We just found him when our dog, Anxious, was hesitant to crawl under the van, and usually it's his favourite spot."

"Aw, what's the matter, little guy?" everyone chorused, the body forgotten for a moment as all eyes turned to Anxious.

Not wanting to miss an opportunity, he lifted his paw, widened his brown orbs, and whined.

"Don't let him fool you. Anxious is his name, not his emotional state, and his paw is fine."

"I think that's for me to decide, sir," growled the officer. "Have you been mistreating this animal?"

"Of course not! I love him. He's my best friend beside Min."

"And who might that be, sir?"

"The woman standing right next to me who you seem to be totally ignoring. Is your eyesight okay?"

Everyone went silent and heads snapped around to stare at me, aghast. Clearly, this particular officer was not someone you were ever meant to answer back to.

"You… Well I never! Have some respect for those who keep you safe at night, sir."

"I have the utmost respect for the police, but I don't respect those who think belittling others is how to behave."

"Good for you, mate," said the male paramedic, then slapped me on the back before joining his colleague.

"I did no such thing. Tell them, Mark." He turned to his colleague, who had the good grace to frown at him. "What did I do?"

"You ignored the lady and acted like she wasn't important. You always do this. How many times do I have to tell you? Stop acting like it's only men in the world."

"It's just my way, you know that. Sir, I apologise." He smiled at me, and held out his hand, whilst everyone else groaned. "What did I do wrong now?"

"Wow, you really don't get it, do you?" asked the young female officer as she stepped forward to join the rest of us.

"Get what?"

"You apologised to the man, not the woman. You should sit this one out, Frank. It's clearly too much for you to handle."

While they bickered, Min and I joined the paramedics as they performed their checks, and Min asked, "Do you know what killed him? He was stuck to the undercarriage. We discovered him when we crawled under with our dog."

"Too early to tell yet, but by the looks of it he broke his neck sometime in the night. He's still warm, but that's just the heat of the day. I wouldn't feel bad, as it clearly wasn't your fault. Most likely, he was trying to sneak in and got a nasty surprise on those stupid speed bumps. They're way too big and hard, and we had a nightmare with the ambulance, so I can only imagine what it was like in the van."

"It was bumpy," I agreed. "Do you think it's suspicious? Anything strange about it? Could he have been put there somehow?"

"I don't see how."

"Me either," agreed her partner. "Looks like he was trying to pull a fast one and not pay the entrance fee. Bit daft, as it's well worth the price. The pie rolling tomorrow is always awesome."

"It's lame," sighed the woman. "Rolling pies into the lake is a waste of good food. They're for eating. Who wants a soggy pie?"

"Don't be such a spoilsport. It's good for the town. It brings in thousands of people and the businesses all make a mint. Plus, the death slide is amazing. Have you tried it?" he asked us.

"It was a blast," said Min. "Max did it out of love, but hated it."

"It's true. It was terrifying."

"You wouldn't catch me risking my life for what passes as fun," said the woman as she packed away her things. "Well, that's us. The detectives will take over from here. Should be along soon. In the meantime, I'd stay out of the way of the old fart. He's from another era and refuses to keep with the times. Thinks women should be in the kitchen and only allowed out on weekends to go shopping. Right nightmare to deal with he is."

"We'll bear it in mind," said Min.

We shook their hands, then watched them leave. I wondered if they'd be back to retrieve the body later, and hadn't thought to ask until it was too late. As Min and I stood and turned away from the body, Frank and Mark stepped forward as one.

"You folks doing okay?" asked Mark with a sympathetic smile.

"We're fine. It's a shock, but we're handling it. We were about to have a coffee. Would you like one?"

"No thank you."

"I'd love one," smirked Frank, seeming to think it was funny for some reason. Most likely, he thought it would inconvenience us.

"Fine," huffed Min, then retreated into the gazebo.

Frank followed her in and slumped into one of the camping chairs, which creaked ominously.

"Frank, get your sorry ass up! What is wrong with you?" demanded Mark with an apologetic shake of his head to me.

"I've been on my feet all day and I'm done for. This is the last thing I need."

"Oh, you poor thing," crooned Min, face full of sympathy.

"Thanks. It's a tough life for us coppers."

Min rolled her eyes at Mark and me, and we both stifled a titter as Frank turned awkwardly in the chair.

"What are you two chuckling about?" he growled, face dark.

"Chill, Frank, but let's face it, this is always an easy gig. Nothing normally ever happens, and we always get this kind of job now. You just like complaining."

"I do not. I served my time, caught my fair share of criminals, and I want to take it easy for the few months before I retire. You only have a few days left, so don't tell me you want to deal with this nonsense. It'll be a nightmare. Two bodies in one day is never good."

"Get up and stop being such an idiot! You know as well as I do that we won't be too involved in things here. Not for us to solve a crime. We'll ask people a few questions, keep them from having a nose, then later on you can return to lazing about and complaining."

"Yeah, you're right. It's not like there's even a crime to solve."

"There you go!" Mark winked at us as Frank heaved from my startled chair, which groaned as it settled back into its usual shape. "I think we have everything we need from you both. It's unfortunate, but these things do happen I'm afraid. You folks okay? Anything we can do? Do you need to see the paramedics? Stress maybe?"

"No, we're fine. What happens now?" asked Min, casting a concerned look my way.

"Now we wait for the detective to come and look over the scene, so I'm afraid in the meantime you'll have to steer clear of the van and the deceased. We'll put some tape around the area, or the youngsters will." He nodded to the two keen officers who got to work straight away, clearly much more excited about something happening than the old-timers.

"Bleedin' nuisance is what this is. Two deaths, and two major headaches," grumbled Frank, eyeing our drinks greedily; neither of us offered him one.

"Sorry to be a bother," I said.

"Yeah, well," he grumbled, "you ought to be more careful."

"Frank here isn't big on understanding sarcasm," laughed Mark, taking his partner's arm and dragging him away.

"I get sarcasm! Guess we better go talk to everyone on the stalls. My brother will be along shortly," he told us as he turned back to us.

"Brother?" I asked.

"Frank's younger brother is a DI. He'll be looking into this to make sure it's on the level. Nothing to worry about. Just the usual formalities. Don't sweat it."

"So, your brother is a detective?" asked Min.

"So what!?" Frank snapped.

Mark winked at us and chuckled. "It's a sore point. Frank here doesn't exactly have the personality or the inclination to rise in the ranks. Can't say I was ever interested. The paperwork is tedious enough as it is just being a copper. Sibling rivalry, eh, Frank?" Mark jabbed his partner in his large stomach, the flesh bouncing. Frank batted his hand away with a deep scowl.

"I could have been a detective if I wanted. Too many exams, though, and they're all so up themselves."

Without another word, they wandered off, arguing and poking each other. We watched them go, stunned and silent, then turned our attention to the keen young officers who had already secured crime scene tape around Vee and tied it to the gazebo, making a cordon around the body.

"Does this mean it is a crime scene?" Min asked them.

"It's just the tape we had. I'm Kim, by the way, and this is Jim. Sorry about those two, especially Frank. He's what you'd call a jaded copper, and hard to like. We steer clear if we can."

"Too right we do," said Jim. "Man's a nightmare. Always complaining, acting like he's hard done by, when they get the easy jobs and he still moans. We want to be out on patrol but got stuck watching over things here, but at least something's happened." He smiled happily, then after a nudge from Kim said, "Of course, it's awful."

"We understand. You're new to the force and want to prove yourselves. It's understandable."

Both removed their hats and wiped their arms across their sweaty foreheads, eyes dancing with excitement and barely contained eagerness. They could have been brother and sister they looked so similar. With Kim's short cropped dark hair, Jim's a sensible copper's buzzcut, clear complexions and wiry frames, they were obviously fresh from the academy and brimming with the energy of youth.

"So far, being on the force has been beyond tame. We've had a few jobs like this and haven't even had to arrest anyone."

"Jim, stop acting so excited. It's not very professional. Sorry about him." Kim beamed at us, then glanced at the body. "Poor bloke. Wonder what happened? Maybe it was a murder."

"You think?" exclaimed Jim. "That would be awesome! Um, not awesome, terribly sad, but it would be cool."

"You really do want some action, don't you?" I laughed, understanding that they were simply keen to prove their worth.

"It would make a change. But I doubt we'll get it. We need to get back to the other scene and check on things, but nice to meet you both."

"You too. Um, do you mind giving Anxious a fuss? I think we might have an exploding dog on our hands otherwise." I nodded to the loitering guy sitting in front of the officers, tail wagging, head cocked, confused by the lack of adoration. Why wasn't he being admired and stroked? It didn't compute in his brain.

"Oh, sorry, little fella," cooed Kim, squatting and adjusting her utility belt, the array of devices always an interest for me. It looked so cool, like Batman, but I doubted they had as many gadgets as him. The truncheons looked like fun though!

"What a lovely dog. We have a Jack Russell at home and he's ace. Always up for a you know what." Jim got on his knees and stroked Anxious behind the ears where he liked it, while Kim rubbed his back. Anxious was in his element, and clearly liked them both, so kept his head high and his tail wagging as they lavished the appropriate amount of attention on the country's best dog as far as he was concerned.

"Are you both local?" I asked.

"A few towns over. They like new cops to be away from their local area, fresh eyes and all that," said Kim as she stood. "But we know the area well, as there isn't exactly a big city around here."

"More sheep than people," agreed Jim. "I've been coming here for years, so has Kim. It's a local tradition. Never seen anything like this before though. Two deaths is not normal. Usually, the worst that happens is there's a fight over whose pie is biggest. You wait until later. They'll be punching the living daylights out of each other."

"Really? It gets that competitive?" I asked.

"You bet," said Kim. "It's their reputation on the line. Means some great business for the whole year. The local pubs and restaurants want to sell the award winner's pies as that's what everyone demands."

"And who won last year?" wondered Min, glancing at me.

"Tim, of course," said Jim happily. "Everyone knows that. Poor guy would have most likely won this year too. Doubt his wife will be up to it now, but you never know. It's like a guarantee of a profitable year."

With a smile, they left, racing away to check on things, no doubt annoying the older officers with their endless chatter and young energy.

"So, Tim and Tina won last year," mused Min, her cheeks dimpling as she smiled, the unmistakable look of mischief and excitement in her eyes.

"They did, and now he's dead. Could it be something besides an accident? And why does the man lying just over there have their business card in his pocket?"

"I think we have some investigating to do." Min clapped her hands together and smiled.

Anxious leapt to his feet and raced laps around us, excited by Min's outburst.

Chapter 5

With our morning not going exactly to plan, the plan being to chill out to the max, no pun intended, the moment we were alone we retreated to the front of the gazebo where we could sit in the sunshine and put our backs to the horrific scene behind us. It was incongruous and downright disconcerting to be left alone with a corpse outside Vee, and neither of us knew what to do. He'd been covered up by the paramedics, but they weren't allowed to move him until the scene had been photographed and the detective had gone over everything to his satisfaction.

After having been involved with so many cases before, I was still unsure if it was right that the police had simply left us to it. Surely someone should have stayed? Nevertheless, we vowed to try and be positive, so stretched out in the chairs and sipped our coffees after I made a fresh brew, the previous drinks having gone cold while we dealt with Frank and his antics.

Watching everyone splashing in the lake, screaming as they descended the death slide, or dragging children along as they complained about being hungry, tired, bored, or over-hyped and excited because of the fun, caused us both to feel rather peculiar. On the one hand two men had died, on the other, it shouldn't stop anyone else enjoying themselves. Unless there was a raving lunatic rampaging around knocking off people left and right, there wasn't much to be done apart from try to salvage what we could from the day.

Easier said than done when there's a mangled corpse not a stone's throw away lying outside your home, but we did our best and slowly relaxed into our usual easy conversation. Soon, even that dried up and we merely sat in companionable silence, watching the world go by, pleased to be in each other's company.

"I can't stand it any longer," I declared, launching to my feet and casting a shadow over Min.

"I'm amazed you lasted this long," she laughed, lowering her sunglasses so she could look over the rims.

"Don't know what you mean," I said, trying to brazen it out.

"Max, you were one of the best chefs in the country and spent years thinking of nothing but food."

"You know I'm sorry about that."

"That's not what I meant. What I meant was that you're a foodie. Always have been, always will be. The fact that you've managed to hold off on buying pies this long is downright incredible. I'm starving, too, even though it's been a morning full of shocks, but I get it. So, go off and buy us pies, and make sure they're nice ones."

"Oh, wow, yes, I will. It smells amazing, and it doesn't seem like the police have shut the stalls down, so it would be rude not to spend some cash and support the local businesses."

"Absolutely. In fact, it would be almost criminal if you didn't wander around with your tongue hanging out and come back with a bag full of pies. Don't forget," she wagged a finger at me, "that it's only Friday. We still have tomorrow and the pie rolling competition, and there will be even more food on offer then, so don't overdo it. Just get what we can eat for lunch and maybe something for dinner unless you're cooking. In fact, don't get dinner. We can always wander around later and pick something up, but a nice cheese pie would be awesome."

"You have a deal. I'll be quick, as I'm famished, unless you want to come too?"

"I'm going to stay right here and sun my legs and relax. You enjoy yourself. Leave the little guy here so he doesn't get into mischief."

"No problem. See you in ten."

"By that, I hope you don't mean ten hours. I know what you're like once you get chatting to people and will want to sample every single one until you decide. Just pick a few pies that look nice and hurry back."

"I'll be quick. Promise."

I glanced quickly at Anxious who was curled up and asleep, so sidled off keeping an eye on him, doing my best to be quiet or he'd definitely want to come. Anxious liked food as much as me, and wasn't as fussy. If it was down to him, he'd spend his pocket money at the first stall, stuff his face, then expect to be given next week's money then conveniently forget about it and complain that he didn't have cash for ice-cream later.

Chuckling to myself about the way I made up little scenarios about the crazy guy, I wandered off and found myself suddenly feeling depressed. It didn't happen often—I was a very positive man who always tried to look on the bright side of life and be thankful for everything I had—but now and then my thoughts turned dark and brooding; I'd learned to let it happen and think it through then move on.

It was because of the way I'd been imagining Anxious and pocket money. It was linked to our inability to have children. We'd accepted that years ago, were reconciled to the fact, and had even discussed adoption but then our relationship had soured and it got put aside. But it was still there, the knowledge that we would never have a little one running around, a child we could take on trips, show the world too, spoil, fuss over, kiss and cuddle, and I knew that it still saddened Min on occasion.

She was enough for me, and I hoped I was enough for her, in fact I knew I was, but there was no doubt we would have both loved a child. Some things simply weren't to be. We did have Anxious, who we both adored, and he was definitely part of our little family, but when I thought of

Min and the huge blow it had been to her, and me, when we found out, I couldn't help but feel for her. I adored her, I truly did, and yet had caused her no end of grief. Although I'd managed to change and become a better man, leaving my old ways far behind me, this was still the one thing that caused her emotional distress that I could do absolutely nothing about.

No amount of words, of promising she was my whole world and made me happier than I could ever explain, could change the fact that we would never have a child of our own.

It broke my heart, because I knew she wished it could be different. She was a brave woman, the absolute best, and I would do anything in my power to make her happy, but at this I could only fail.

Shaking my head, I paused and looked out at the lake, and laughed quietly to myself. This was dumb. It was what it was and there was zero point dwelling on it. We were closer than ever, even closer than we were when first married, and our relationship brought me so much joy. It clearly did for Min too. She was happier than I'd seen her in many years, and that was down to me no longer being a selfish, egotistical, obsessive idiot. We had nothing to complain about and a whole glorious future to look forward to unless she decided that after considering things she didn't want us to be together again. My stomach flipped at the thought, but again I laughed, knowing it was just my mind trying to cause me pain when deep down I knew the truth.

We loved each other and were destined to be together. Feeling better about things, and knowing sometimes it was best not to listen to your own mind as for some reason on occasion it turned into your enemy rather than your friend with ridiculous thoughts and dumb ideas, taking you away from the present moment and dwelling on things impossible to do anything about, I focused on the here and now and lifted my face to the glorious sun.

What a day to be alive. How beautiful. People having fun. Playing, talking, eating. There was no reason to feel blue, but every reason to rejoice. My spirits lifted until I felt weightless and free like I couldn't explain, and when I came back to myself it was with a renewed vow to do anything I could to ensure Min was happy.

"Pies, that's what she needs. Some lovely pies." Whistling, I hurried back onto the path that led along the line of stalls where most people were now eager to get their lunch, and so began my search for the perfect lunch pie.

Skirting the stall where Tim had died as it was shut anyway, I checked out the wares of the main makers, marvelling at the robust, golden pastry, the decorative crusts, the smells, and sampled several without overdoing it. I kept conversation with the vendors brief, mindful that Min was waiting, but it was impossible not to catch snippets of conversation, all concerning Tim and his unfortunate demise.

As I did the rounds, one thing became more than apparent. All the artisans knew each other, there was an incredible amount of rivalry, and although people were sad Tim had passed, there was an undeniable air of excitement now the competition was freed up and last year's winner was out of the picture. I heard people talking about how much business High Pies had got since winning, and they were eager to get a slice of the action. It would make them a mint for a year with more orders than they could fulfil, so the competitors were falling over themselves to make the greatest giant pie as a way of showcasing their skills. After all, if you could make a huge pie that tasted incredible, you could be sure that regular sized ones would be even better.

What also became very apparent was that there was no love lost between most of them and High Pies. Whereas quite a few adjacent businesses were getting along well, competitive but all in good spirits despite the potential reward, there wasn't much sadness over Tim's death, or that much sympathy for Tina, his wife. Muttered comments under people's breath about good riddance and that he most likely had a heart attack because he was so highly strung were common, even though they did their best to keep their opinions quiet and not talk bad of the dead in front of customers.

I understood where many were coming from, as it had been the same in restaurants. Most chefs were nice enough, but their obsession made them disagreeable, easy to anger, and often very demanding. High Pies had gone through a number of staff that didn't connect with the business, as they catered exclusively to the festival scene and local businesses, without running a shop of their own. Most of the others functioned in similar ways. Less overheads, guaranteed custom at festivals, fetes, or corporate events, and focused on production from kitchens of all sizes without the horrendous overheads of a shop to maintain and staff.

I was actually quite envious, and had to catch myself as I began to daydream about a little operation making bespoke pies or something similar, maybe pork pies or sausage rolls, and building an empire. Then I could expand, and have outlets all over the country supplying local pubs and restaurants. That's where I caught myself, and shook my head in wonder at the absurdity of it all. Why on earth would I want to do that? I had my freedom, I could cook every night in my cast-iron pot to satisfy the need to make lovely meals, and I had Min and Anxious to consider. Stress levels would rise, I'd get focused to the detriment of everything else, and it would lead to nothing but another personal disaster. No thank you very much!

Grunting in satisfaction for having had a sensible word with myself, I completed the rounds of the stalls, having reigned in my chef side and gone for only three cheese and onion pies with local herbs, a few bottles of local cider, several tubs of pasta salads that I was assured, and became convinced by a sample, were out of this world, and some little tubs of herby roast potatoes with Parmesan shavings that were a genuine surprise and something I would definitely be making myself.

Keening to return to Min and Anxious, hoping the detectives and assorted teams would have been and gone and we could be done with the whole sorry affair, I nevertheless strolled leisurely back to our pitch, enjoying the sunshine and the happy vibes of the festival atmosphere, thinking about other events to come later this year.

There would be Lydstock, which was a must, especially as Uncle Ernie was playing again this year, several other small music festivals, and I also fancied going to Green Man but had failed to get tickets as it had become shockingly popular. Still, there was always End of the Road, a real music lovers festival, so maybe I'd invite Min to that. Anxious always enjoyed it when we used to go as the wide open spaces, the freedom it afforded, the laid back atmosphere, and the play area in the woods were ideal for youngsters.

Humming to myself happily, I turned past a group of campervans, ducked around a group of people in the path chatting away about the pie competition, then approached our pitch.

Min had her back to me, standing next to a bulky man in a drab grey suit and greying, thin hair that he brushed back repeatedly. Anxious was facing me, keeping a look out, taking his guard duty seriously while Min was with a stranger, and it made me smile. I leaned over and patted my legs and he came tearing over then leaped into my outstretched arms, tongue already lapping, tail wagging, as pleased to see me as if I'd been gone for weeks.

"Hey, buddy, you're such a good boy. I got us some lovely treats, so let's have lunch soon, eh?"

A merry bark was all the confirmation I needed that he was ready to eat, not that he would ever turn down a meal.

After he calmed a little, I released him and he hurried back over and resumed his position. Something about his body language and the fact he was ignoring them gave me pause, so I approached cautiously, stepped past him, and moved up beside Min. She smiled wanly as I nudged her, then shook her head.

Confused, I turned to the man beside her, a burly guy of six foot, grossly overweight, his XXL suit and shirt bulging in all the wrong places. His tie was crooked, like he just couldn't be bothered to do it properly. A ruddy complexion spoke of years of unhealthy eating and too much alcohol, and the smell made it obvious he'd been indulging today already. I took another sniff and moved closer to Min, having never in my life smelled a man that stank so bad. He hadn't showered for a long time, his clothes certainly hadn't been laundered this century, and deodorant wasn't a word he'd ever come across.

"Hi, I'm Max. I assume you're Frank's brother."

The DI turned to me, his movements almost glacial, zero expression on his face, and held up a huge, podgy hand right in my face and shook his head.

I glanced at Min and she merely shrugged.

"Look, I don't know what—"

Again with the hand.

Deciding I simply couldn't be bothered with this nonsense, and not letting this fool get to me and ruin my mood, I took the approach of it was his problem not mine so smiled at Min and asked if she wanted to have lunch.

"Oh, yes, so much," she gushed, shaking her head as she indicated with her head the peculiar man beside us. We left him staring at the body and returned to the gazebo.

"What's that all about?" I whispered as I busied myself with unwrapping the goodies and Min sorted out plates and cutlery.

"Bloke's super weird. Wouldn't let me speak, and just introduced himself then told me to be quiet. He makes his brother, Frank, seem like a sweetie." Min leaned in close and said, "He gives me the creeps."

"He's definitely an odd one. Hey, maybe he's solving the case!"

"Doubt it. He's more concerned with getting another drink by the smell of him."

"Then forget about him and let's eat. What do you think?" I placed pies and other treats on the table and stepped back. "I did good, right?"

"Very good." Min licked her lips and smiled before standing on tiptoe and kissing my cheek. "And you got cider too? Great!"

We cut everything up so we could sample it all, gave Anxious some treats, then settled in our chairs and tucked in. Talking in whispers, we'd glance around every so often to check on the DI, but he hadn't moved a muscle. It was disconcerting, and beyond rude, and made it impossible to relax, but we tried our best, and by the time we'd begun on the pies we'd forgotten about him and were enjoying our lunch.

Then he came over, blotting out the sun as he stood in front of the view, and frowned as he stared down at us like we'd done something wrong.

Chapter 6

Min and I shook our heads in wonder at the incredible rudeness of this humongous man. I'd encountered numerous surly, grumpy, sometimes downright hostile members of our police force over the last nine months or so, but this guy took the biscuit. In fact, he nabbed the whole pack!

He continued to merely stare, and for a moment a stab of guilt washed over me—was he deaf? Mute? Then I recalled that he'd spoken briefly to Min, so the simple fact was he didn't care and was playing some kind of game. Well, I didn't want to play, so rather than get annoyed, I took Min's empty plate and glass, got up, put hers and mine in the washing-up bowl, topped off our ciders and added ice, then resumed my seat. We chinked glasses childishly—we were showing off—but this bloke brought out our silly side as it had become like a bad comedy. Was he trying to intimidate us?

Finally, I'd had enough.

"Look, mate, you're blocking the sun. Mind standing to the side while you loom and do whatever else it is you think you're doing? I'd like to watch people having fun in the lake, not stare at you."

"And if you don't mind," added Min, "I'd rather you stopped staring at my legs. I could report you for that."

His eye twitched, and his cheeks reddened as he shuffled to his left. Anxious followed with a turn of his head, as intrigued as us as to what he would do next.

He continued to stand and stare, but at me exclusively. Several more minutes passed, and I was about to get up and shove the fool into the lake as I'd had enough. What was he playing at? This was no way to treat people. Just as I began to move, he put out a hand to stop me, then retrieved his phone with the other and turned it so I could see the screen. It was my wiki page that Dad kept updated.

"Just no," he said. "Absolutely not. I've gone over everything, and this case, and the other, is closed. Tim had a heart attack, I'm sure, although there will be an autopsy to confirm, and the man under your van died because he was an idiot."

"Wait one minute!" I rose, but he stormed forward and shoved me back into my chair. I was so shocked I didn't even try to get up. Anxious raced from my side, stood in front of me and growled, his teeth bared. His hackles were up and I'd never seen him look quite as menacing. He might have been small, but he could tear flesh from even this man's frame, and cause real damage. Once he got hold, he would not let go.

The DI stepped back, glared at Anxious who lost a little of his bravado, but nevertheless remained guarding us, albeit in a more quiet manner.

"I don't want to hear a word. You may think you're a hotshot amateur detective, but not on my watch. Whoever this guy is died because he was trying to get in for free. End of. I'm not going to spend my day traipsing around this hellhole talking to a bunch of losers only to end up right back where I started. Accidental death by misadventure. Case closed."

"What's your name?" I asked, my heart hammering, but outwardly I was calm.

"My name is Detective Inspector Mike Almond."

"Almond? That's unusual," noted Min.

"No, it isn't. Now, are we clear? You are not to interfere. You will not ask questions, you will stay away from those concerned with this matter, there will be no talking to the officers, and you will be sorry if you try to interfere. I won't have this turned into a circus."

"You haven't even inspected the body properly. You just stood there," said Min, clearly exasperated.

"I'm forty years on the force. I know what I'm doing and have seen this countless times before. The case is closed. No murder, no foul play, just a heart attack and an unfortunate accident because of one man's stupidity. We are done."

Without even a nod, he turned and lumbered off, elbows out wide, barging past anyone foolish enough not to move out of his way, like he owned the world.

Min and I burst out laughing.

When we'd recovered, and Anxious had finished rolling around on his back, kicking his legs out in celebration, I told Min, "That was the weirdest encounter I've ever had. Was he on the level? Think he's really like that?"

"Yes, I do. You should have seen him when he first arrived. He did the hand thing, didn't say a word, just stood there until you came. It was freaking me out."

"I bet it was! Wow, that was so weird. You can see the family resemblance to Frank. He and Mike are definitely brothers."

"Yes, but Mike made Frank seem like a sweetie. What happens now? The case is really closed?"

"Looks that way. I get that he put Tim's death down to a heart attack, but to dismiss the guy under Vee as an accident without even knowing who he is or what he was doing under there seems downright strange, bordering on negligent."

"I wonder if he'll even try to find out who he is?"

"I wouldn't count on it. He didn't seem the type to bother. Maybe he'll get the officers to ask around, see if anyone's missing, but my guess is that he's done with the case apart from writing up a report and filing it. So weird," I repeated, unable to process the man's negativity and dismissive nature, not to mention his incredible rudeness.

"How has he remained a DI for so long with an attitude like that?" Min eyed the remaining food and her stomach rumbled.

"I have no idea. Maybe he's actually a good detective when he can be bothered. Maybe he coasts along and does just enough to keep his job, or maybe they can't get rid of him." My own stomach rumbled and I knew I couldn't hold out much longer. "Shall we have a second lunch? I'm still starving."

"Yes, let's do it! It was so nice, and still smells amazing. You chose well."

"Anxious seems to think so," I agreed, nodding to the little guy who had switched from guarding us to protecting our leftovers from any marauding pie thieves. He glanced our way when we laughed, then his head snapped back around to focus on the table laden with my remaining purchases.

Eager to put the peculiar encounter with the detective behind us, and still bewildered by the whole bizarre encounter, we launched eagerly from our seats and headed for the table. We managed a single step before someone called out, "Hello?"

We turned to find the two paramedics from earlier standing looking rather awkward at the entrance to the gazebo, a stretcher between them, and a crowd of onlookers just behind, the draw of their presence stronger than the lure of pies, or so it seemed.

"Sorry to disturb you again, but we've come to take the body, if that's okay?" The man glanced at his partner, both of them looking uncomfortable.

"Of course," I said, a sense of relief washing over me. "Don't forensics teams or photographers need to come first?"

"Apparently not." He shrugged, but the look on his face told a thousand words.

"It's okay, we get it," said Min, smiling in sympathy. "I'm assuming you've had dealings with Mike Almond before?"

"Quite a few times," said the woman. "He's, how do I put this, rather a unique man."

"You can say that again," grunted her partner. "He says the scene's done with and we can take away the deceased, so if that's alright, we will."

"You go ahead." I nodded, and led them over, not that they needed the help.

Without preamble, they loaded the man carefully onto the stretcher after zipping him into a body bag, which was never a nice sight, and always made things seem too final. With grim nods and awkward smiles, they carried him the short distance over to where the ambulance had been parked, the crowds dispersing after watching the scene with a mix of curiosity and sadness.

As they drove off, and everyone returned to their own business, Min and I stood for a while in silence, staring at the spot where the mystery man had been laying, everything odd because it now appeared normal. With no sign of anything untoward having ever happened, it was eerie because as far as those in charge were concerned, this was now done with, at least for us. It would obviously be a while before Tim's cause of death was confirmed, so it was doubtful we'd even hear about it, and as for the man from under Vee, I was at a loss as to what to think.

"What should we do now?" I wondered.

"There's only one thing for it." Min turned to me and smiled, took my hand and squeezed, then suggested, "Shall we eat? It feels wrong to get on with our day after what's happened, but what else can we do?"

"You're right, let's finish up here then decide what comes next."

"And what exactly are you thinking that might be?"

"I'm not sure, but a man is dead, two men actually, and I can't shake the feeling that this is far from right. We owe the guy we found the right to at least be named, and to figure out what happened for him to end up stuck under our campervan. It's wrong to leave it like this with no answers."

"You're right, and we will, but first let's settle our nerves by pigging out on pie. It's not disrespectful, as we genuinely care, not like that horrid DI, but right now we need to eat."

"Sounds like the perfect plan."

With Anxious overseeing preparations yet again, ensuring no crumbs got overlooked, and no pies were harmed in the making of our lunch, we quickly prepared everything then settled down, eager to sample the remaining wares.

"It's okay," I told Min as she stared at her plate of food but didn't eat. "You're allowed to enjoy your food."

"It feels wrong, like we're insulting the dead. How long was he under Vee for, Max? How awful was it for him? How can the DI be so dismissive of something like this? I don't understand."

"Neither do I," I admitted, glancing over to where we'd dragged him. "But you can count on one thing, and that's that we won't be as cold and uncaring as Mike Almond. I still can't believe that guy. Come on, eat up, then maybe we'll do a little digging and see what we can uncover. It might be as the detective said and it was an unfortunate accident, but we need to find out enough to salve our own conscience."

"Thanks. That sounds good. Not good, but... Oh, you know what I mean!" Min threw up her arms in despair, which Anxious took as a sign that she didn't want her lunch, so he sat before her, tail swishing the ground, eyes full of hope.

"In your dreams, mister," I laughed, shaking my head at his boundless optimism.

The food was even more delicious the second time around as there was no Mike Almond to sour the mood, and we both ate with gusto once we got going and tried to focus on the good rather than the bad, and the remaining pie was a revelation. For such a simple thing, they were packed full of flavour with some surprise ingredients that made them surpass what you would generally get in a cheese and potato pie, and I managed to figure out a few ingredients that I would be sure to use in the future.

But the whole meal was tinged with the unmistakable cloud of death, and there was no avoiding it. We were quieter than usual, certainly less upbeat, and I think it was more the attitude of the authorities than anything else. It's the one thing you hope you can rely on. That if bad things happen, those who have vowed to protect you, to get justice, will do all they can to assist.

Having to deal with Frank, the rude cop, and his brother, the bewildering detective, had left a sour taste in our mouths. That wasn't how they were meant to be. They were supposed to care, to want to help people, not be dismissive and act like they simply couldn't be bothered. It tested your faith in things you were meant to be able to trust absolutely. I knew they were people the same as us, but those who chose such a profession should know better. If nothing else, their own conscience should have made them do what they could to get justice for those who deserved it, or at least want to ensure they had a clear picture of what'd really happened. Didn't they care at all? It didn't seem like it.

I cleared away the kitchen while Min sorted out a few bits and pieces, and when we were done we moved our chairs into the sun and sat back down, both craving warmth and the cheer of the light and heat. For a while, we watched people playing in the lake and screaming their way down the death slide, the happy vibe lifting us from our funk, and soon we became more animated, chuckling at people's antics, slowly overheating, until our conversation was back to normal and we were both smiling, the events of the morning fading enough to let us put things into perspective.

Leaving Min to sun herself, I stood and stretched out, my body aglow with energy from the sunbathing, the delicious sunshine, and the happy atmosphere buzzing around the site. Suddenly feeling antsy, I wandered over to Vee, noting the strange graffiti on the side of the van, wondering what on earth it meant, and why someone had done it on several occasions. The mystery of it continued to annoy me on occasion, as I couldn't figure out why someone had done it, or even how. Another stalker? Or was it more than one person and a copycat had seen the beginnings of the mysterious artwork and decided to have a go too? Something else that made no sense? I'd grown accustomed to it now and had merely let it be, somehow understanding that this mystery would reveal itself in good time.

What currently occupied my thoughts was much more important anyway, and that was how the man had been under Vee. With curiosity getting the better of me, I glanced back to make sure Min wasn't watching, as I didn't want to upset her further, then got onto all fours before lying down and sliding under. I figured this was the best way to get a feel for what it was like under her, as there was no other way of knowing.

What became obvious immediately, and was something I already knew, was that there was next to no space underneath the camper to manoeuvre. The van was slung rather low, hence me often wincing when I drove over rough country lanes and bottomed out, so how the man managed to slide under, cling on, and keep himself raised off the ground at least for a while was a real head-scratcher.

I crawled further under until I was where he had been found, and with a little shifting about I managed to find where I believed he must have hung on. There were a surprising number of handholds to get your fingers into, and some good spots to wedge your feet in, but I couldn't help thinking that it would be unbearably hot with the heat from the exhaust, and that was before you even considered the danger involved. Getting a good grip, and with my Crocs squeezed into the best footholds I could find, I pulled myself up so I was raised off the ground; my arms began to scream immediately.

The slightest bump would see me slamming into the ground and my back rubbed raw, just like the mystery man's, but then the question arose of how on earth he managed to remain hanging on under such conditions. It didn't seem possible. He'd be banged about so much that he'd surely let go and most likely get run over by the rear wheels. He hadn't been a super fit looking guy, so his strength would have run out almost immediately, and even if it hadn't, the rough ride would have dislodged him. It wasn't like he'd been tied on or anything.

I dropped to the grass with a sigh and a moan, more in the dark about the whole thing than ever, then slid out, aghast at the blood and oil and general grime covering my hands after only a few seconds. It was his blood, not mine, which was odd, but to be expected I assumed, or should it have been there where he was holding on? Maybe he caught a knuckle or something but kept his grip?

After washing my hands thoroughly and brushing myself down, I stood and stared at Vee, trying to come up with a sensible explanation, but drew a blank. None of this computed. Why hadn't anyone looked underneath properly to ensure the man could have actually been holding on while I drove? But that then begged the question, what really happened? Had he become trapped under there somehow so couldn't escape? That would explain the damage he'd received. If he hadn't got himself stuck, he would have let go within seconds. No way could any normal person stay put.

"Max."

I turned at Min's call to find the woman from the pie stall who had first discovered Tim standing beside her, red-faced, wringing her hands, and shifting from foot to foot.

"Hi," I said, an eyebrow raised in question to Min. She shrugged.

"Sorry to disturb you, but I think we have a lot to talk about," stammered the woman. "Tim's dead, and I think it was murder. And I hear a man died here too. It's no coincidence. I can tell you that much."

"Then you better take a seat," I said, trying to mask my sigh by raising my hand to my mouth and smoothing down my beard.

Chapter 7

"It's Kelly, right?" I noted the black ponytail, and her branded apron, surprised I recalled the name after so many new faces this morning.

"Yes. And I know who you both are. I was sure I recognised you, so checked online. Max and Min, the famous detectives, with their handsome sidekick, Anxious. Hey, buddy, how are you? How's your paw?" She turned to me and explained, "I read about his paw on the wiki page. It's very detailed."

"Yes, Dad likes to share more than is strictly necessary. Much more. Our personal life is seemingly an open book now."

"It is very comprehensive. I'm sure you two will make a go of it. Are you close to getting back together?" Kelly seemed oblivious to the fact some things were personal and not to be discussed with total strangers, but she was a nice girl, or woman, I supposed, and very friendly.

"Let's just say we're working on it," I laughed, glancing at Min and shaking my head. She smiled back, clearly having taken to her too.

I retrieved the spare chair from the back of Vee, ignoring the growing number of things rammed into the too small space, vowing to address the mess soon, then we sat. Anxious launched into Kelly's lap, most likely having heard her ask about his leg. He balanced on her thighs, lifted a paw, and whined.

"He's a cheeky scamp, isn't he?" With a laugh, Kelly shook the offered limb and told him, "I won't fall for that, but you can have a head rub if you want?"

Anxious barked that it was agreeable given the circumstances, which seemed to include a distinct lack of biscuits, so Kelly fulfilled her promise and he soon curled up. He clearly liked her.

"Kelly, why did you say Tim was murdered? You don't think it was a heart attack?"

"Of course not. That's why I'm here. He was as fit as a fiddle, certainly fitter than me, and he was only early forties. Never had any issues with his health, and suddenly he keels over into the pie, dead? Makes no sense."

"Things like that do happen all the time," said Min softly.

"Not often, but yeah, I get that it could happen. The only issue is that he had no history of illness. How many perfectly healthy people die of heart attacks? Not many, I can tell you. I looked it up."

"Did you say this to the police?" I asked.

"Of course I did! But that utter weirdo of a detective would have none of it. Said I was hysterical and making no sense. Utter nut job he was. Hardly spoke, more like grunts, and didn't want to talk to me. He spoke to Tina, that's Tim's wife, a little, but she got the same stubborn, couldn't care less attitude. She reckons it was murder too. Mike Almond said there was no sign of anything dodgy and no reason to suspect anything untoward, and we should stop being crybabies."

"He actually said that?" I was aghast, but it didn't surprise me.

"He did. Poor Tina fell to bits. She's an utter mess. They took Tim away and she went with them, although I'm not sure there's anything she can do. They have to do a postmortem, which she wasn't happy about, but I suppose at least it means they're looking into things."

"She's convinced it was foul play too?" asked Min. I turned to her, eyebrows raised, a smirk on my face. "What?"

"Foul play? What is this, the Famous Five?"

"You know what I mean," she snapped, winking at me. "Kelly, are you sure? It's awful he died, but there's no reason to think it was anything but an unfortunate heart attack, is there?"

"Of course there is. Don't you know what's at stake today? The contest can make or break a business. We won last year, and will win again this year. I won't let anyone stop us. Everyone's after us. Tim and Tina even got death threats the other month. They were told to pull out of the competition and not to come this year."

"Did they take it seriously?" I asked. "Did you inform the police?"

"They laughed it off. We all did. They even had threatening phone calls. Most of the other pie makers are nice enough, but there's no doubt that they want to win. Some more than others. Everyone knows how well the business did this last year, and it's been incredible. It's all down to the pie competition."

"Why does it mean so much? Surely a giant pie doesn't mean the regular sized ones will be lovely." Min shrugged, waiting for an explanation.

For some reason, Kelly seemed to take it as a personal insult. Her mouth opened and closed as her eyes grew wide, but no words came. When she recovered, she asked, "Are you serious?"

"She is," I told her. "Why don't you explain?"

"Min, it's about the reputation and the interest. There are literally hundreds of independent pie makers in the country, but only a few anyone has heard of. If you get your name out there, people take notice, so it's you they choose. Restaurants and even delis will always pick someone they've heard of, especially someone who won a competition like this. It's the biggest and best in the country, especially the last few years since they got the campervan crowd on side. It's been perfect, as people in vans are always looking for great food they don't have to cook, so that alone has upped business a lot. And don't forget this competition isn't just about size. The pie has to taste incredible too. Ours always do, and we've won numerous times over the years. Not the year before last, but we came a close second, but last year we nailed it. The business made a fortune by our standards, and we were on track to beat that this year. A two-year-in-a-row winner will be even more in demand."

"Sounds fair enough," said Min. "You talk like it's your business too. Is that right? You don't just work for the owners?"

"High Pies was my idea years ago. I'm the daughter of Tina's bestie, and they were talking about struggling to make ends meet with a little shop they had on the high street. I suggested pies as who doesn't love a pie? I'd not long finished catering school and was looking for a job. I couldn't invest much money, but Dad loaned me a few thousand so we could pitch in together and get the equipment we needed. The business built from there. The three of us are equal owners, and I'm very proud of what we've done. I'm twenty-five and have my own successful business, earn good money, but I work incredibly hard for it and the hours are a killer. Especially doing the festivals, which is where the real money is at alongside regular orders from restaurants and shops. We put our whole lives into this, and I will not see it ruined by some maniac."

"That's admirable." I was genuinely impressed they'd accomplished so much and come so far, and understood how hard they must have worked to achieve it, but I also lamented the loss of any free time, and hoped they hadn't gone down the route I had and ignored what was really important in life, rather than chasing fame and money. "But let's get real here. None of that really explains why he was killed. I understand rivals might try to stop you winning, but murder? And right at your stall? It's not very likely, is it?"

"Maybe not, but I'm convinced. I just told you we had death threats and weird phone calls. What more do you want? Will you help? Please? And what about the man found at your van? What happened?"

"We won't say no, or yes, yet. We need to think about this first. But let us tell you about the man we found and see if it rings any bells. Maybe you could help to figure out our problem."

"I'll certainly try." Kelly leaned forward, eyes eager, and rubbed her hands together. "So, come on, spill the beans. What happened?"

We explained in as much detail as we could everything that had happened since we first found the body, leaving nothing out. When we'd finished, Kelly leaned back, closed her eyes, and hummed to herself for the longest time. It went on and on, and we grew concerned that she'd slipped into a trance, and maybe needed her meds, but then her eyes snapped open and she grinned. Her dark eyes caught the sun and sparkled, the lashes even brighter as the mascara must have contained something to make them do that; all I could think of was a child caught getting into mischief.

"What is it?" gasped Min, jumping to her feet, Kelly's excitement clear.

"Do you know something?" I wondered.

"Maybe. Give me a minute to put the pieces together. I think you guys are going to love this. Um, sorry, not love, as it's awful what happened, but I think I might be on to something." Kelly closed her eyes again and hummed. I glanced past her to the happy people risking life and limb on the death slide, and couldn't help note the polar opposites of what we were doing to them. Kelly's eyes opened a moment later and she grinned. "It must be connected. It has to be. Tim's brother hasn't been around for ages, and he's a super flaky guy. Always into trouble and asking for money. He used to work for us, but we had to let him go as he was too unreliable. Caused a lot of friction, but we're over it now. I'm betting it's him. Do you have a photo? Oh, his name's Tank."

"Was he a big guy?" I asked, recalling that the dead man wasn't.

"No, he was called Tank because he always wore a tank top over his shirt. Basically, a sleeveless jumper. It was his thing. Thought it made him look menacing, like a gangster or something, but it just made him look weird."

Min and I gasped, and Min grinned as she moved beside me while I played with my phone and got up the pictures I'd taken of the man. "They're quite gruesome, but if there's a chance it is Tank I guess you need to look. Let me get one of just his face so it's not too disturbing."

"I can handle it. Just show me." Kelly clenched her jaw as she came over to stand beside me, then crouched to take a look at the photo I got up on my phone. "That's him! That's Tank. The dumb idiot got himself and Tim murdered, I bet. He probably owed someone money and this is what they did for him not paying. Idiot! He's been nothing but bad luck for Tim ever since they were little kids. Always getting into trouble. He practically disowned him after we fired him as Tim had put up with his nonsense for too long. Guess he did something super dumb and now this has happened."

"You're absolutely sure it's Tank?" I asked, although the tank top and her confirmation really were enough.

"Course I am." Kelly toyed with her ponytail and chewed the end, a deep frown creasing her otherwise line-free face. Her brown eyes closed as she cast her gaze down, then she spat out her hair and suddenly lifted her head. "We must get justice. They deserve it. Sure, Tank was a loser, but I kinda liked him. He was one of those guys, you know? The lovable rogue. It's how he managed to stay working for us for so long. Everyone liked him, but we despaired at the same time."

"When did he leave?" asked Min.

"About a year ago. Just over a year, I guess. Before we won here last year. He didn't take it well and stopped talking to us for months after we let him go. Tim was the one who fired him, so he got the brunt of it, but Tank came around eventually."

"What did he do for money once he had no work?" I asked.

"He bummed around like he always did. Worked a few different jobs for a while, but he was never good at keeping them. He'd always turn up late, go on benders and not bother to go in at all, or when he did go he would always slack off. I heard the same story from every place he worked. He was a loser. Same as he was when he worked for us. Nobody has heard from him for a while, but that's normal. He'd vanish for days, weeks, sometimes months without a word and everyone would worry, then he'd turn up and act like nothing happened. It was just his way."

"So he didn't have a home?" Min glanced at my phone and shuddered, then focused on Kelly. "Nowhere you could go to check if he was alright?"

"He was a vanlifer. Like you, Max. Difference being, he couldn't even get that together properly. He moved into a huge Transit years ago, a right rust bucket of a thing he got cheap from a guy in the pub he barely knew. He was full of plans for how he'd convert it, where he'd go, and had fanciful ideas about starting up a YouTube channel and making loads of money once he got the channel huge and had loads of followers. Idiot never even got around to buying a camera, let alone figuring out how to edit or upload videos. A dreamer, that's what he was. A lovable, annoying, insufferable, kind-hearted fool of a dreamer."

"What a shame. I know vanlife sounds romantic, but unless you have money behind you to get started and a way to earn a living if you're young, then there's no way to do it. Same as living in a house. You need money. Not a lot, as it's very cheap if you don't use campsites, but everyone still has to eat."

"Exactly! That's what everyone told him, but he had his head in the clouds as usual. Wouldn't listen to anyone, and bought the van. It didn't work out quite as he'd planned, of course, but at least he always had a roof over his head. He didn't do a good conversion though. Tried to do it on the cheap rather than properly, which is fine, but it ended up being a freezing cold shell with a bed and a load of cheap cupboards he got for free."

"He didn't insulate the interior, or use any stretch carpet? What about a floor? He must have put a new one down and maybe ply-lined the walls. What about cooking?"

"He did some things right. Yes, he got enough money for a new floor, and even a roll of lino, but no, there was no insulation, just boards he got for cheap, and no carpet or anything on the walls like you see in so many conversions."

"You seem to know a lot about it," noted Min.

"That's because I'm like Max here. I have a Sprinter. It's old, a bit rough around the edges, but I did the conversion properly. Been a few years for me now. The business did alright, but it was still a struggle to pay bills and a mortgage, so I switched to the van and converted it myself. It's awesome and I'd never go back to living in a house now. It makes it easy to travel to festivals, which is still our main earner, especially music festivals. I have a warm, tiny home on wheels, and it suits me perfectly. We don't have a shop, just our factory unit where we cook, so sometimes I sleep in the car park. Other times I drive off somewhere nice, and we're always off to one event or another anyway so it makes sense for me. Max, would you ever go back to living in a house?"

It was an important question, and one I'd thought about many times ever since I gave up my old life. Min was clearly keen on hearing the answer, too, and leaned forward in her chair, studying me rather more closely than was comfortable. "Cards on the table?" Both women nodded. "I love vanlife, and adore the freedom, the ability to go where I want, do what I want, and not have to worry about maintaining a home, but if Min wanted to settle somewhere, I would."

"But would you resent me if we did that?" Min was very serious, and I thought she was about to cry, but then she smiled at me, her cheeks dimpling, and I knew the truth of it in my heart.

"No, never. I understand this life isn't for everyone, and know it's a struggle and a major hassle at times. You have to consider everything from your water to the toilets to coping with a tiny fridge and a million other things. I would be happy anywhere if it was with you."

"Max, that is so kind. Thank you. I do adore Vee, though, and it's so much fun travelling and seeing so many cool places. It's being outdoors that is the real draw though. It's like a never-ending challenge, but in a good way It makes me feel more capable, like I can do anything, and yes, it is cramped and annoying at times, but I love it."

"So…?" I asked, leaving the question hanging like it had been for so long now.

Kelly smiled, her eyes twinkling with excitement as she turned to Min and waited for her answer.

"So, let's find the killer and Max and I can discuss this at another time."

Kelly laughed and said, "Spoilsport."

Min looked into my eyes and smiled. I had my answer.

Chapter 8

"Sorry. I didn't mean for this to get so personal. That's your private business, not mine. And right now we have other things to think about anyway. What's the plan, eh? It's no coincidence that Tank and Tim both die on the same morning, and at the pie festival. It simply has to be related. I can't believe that dumb detective, and the other officers. How come it takes us literally five minutes to find a link but they turned up nothing?"

"Because they didn't want the deaths to be related," said Min. "That Mike Almond just wanted to get away from here as soon as he could. He didn't want to have to deal with a murder investigation. But look, and I don't want this to sound heartless or anything, but now we know who the man was under the van, we need to tell the police and leave it to them."

We both turned to her, shocked. "You're serious?" I asked.

"No way!" hissed Kelly, fists clenched. "Tim's dead, and he was a good guy. I'm not letting that idiot ruin the investigation. We can do a better job than Mike."

"We?" I asked, eyebrows raised.

"Damn straight! I'm more involved than you. It's my business that will suffer. I have to get the pie finished as the competition is in an hour, and Tina's not around. No way am I letting his death be for nothing. Sure, we have to tell the cops, but then what? The detective will most likely find a lame excuse as to why it still isn't murder, and then what? Nothing, that's what. He'll just waddle off and forget about us."

"You're going ahead with the competition?" I was surprised, but also understood how important this was to Kelly and the business, and knew I'd most likely react in the same way. Sometimes you have to carry on no matter what, and although she was clearly close to Tim, she wasn't hit as hard as his family would be.

"Of course I am! Tina and I make a great team and we'll manage somehow, as long as she still wants to be part of the business."

"Think she might leave and not get involved?" I asked.

"Maybe. She isn't into it like me and Tim. She does the work and is great, but she doesn't have the same passion. I live for pies, so did Tim."

"Then I'm sure you'll keep the business going and do very well today," said Min, putting a hand to Kelly's bare arm, her fair skin reddening already in the sun. "You better get covered up or put sunscreen on before you burn."

"Yes, I haven't had a chance what with the upset. I need to get back to the stall now and finish the pie, but please say you'll help. Please?"

"We will. Give us time to think about this, and I don't mean to be rude, but we are here to enjoy ourselves. I know that's hard for you, as it's so personal, and of course it's a terrible thing that happened, but we are just regular people who want to relax."

"Yes, of course. I'm so sorry. This isn't down to you, I know that. It was just when I recognised you I got my hopes up. I'm sorry. You enjoy your day, and don't let me ruin it. But you will think about it?" Kelly stood, her sweat building as she waited nervously for an answer. Anxious jumped from her arms where she was cradling him and landed in front of us then cocked his head, waiting for our answer.

Min smiled and confirmed, "Yes, we'll help. How could we not? But as Max said, we do want to enjoy the day too. Gosh, that sounds awful. We aren't bad people, Kelly, but we haven't had much time together lately and wanted to have a fun few days. You understand?"

"I do, and it's so sweet. You guys are made for each other. Max, like your dad said on your wiki page, I hope you don't mess this up."

I sighed and said, "So do I, but I wish he'd stopped sharing so much information with total strangers."

"I think it's sweet," said Min, squeezing my arm. "He's just looking out for you, and of course they think I'm great!"

"You are great," I agreed.

"Get a room!" Kelly rolled her eyes and smiled, then with a nod she left, leaving us with an awful lot to think about. She turned back and called out, "I'll call the detective. I have his number. Guess he might come back to talk to us, but I wouldn't count on it."

We watched her go, Min with barely contained excitement. Once she was out of sight, Min jumped to her feet and declared, "We already have a great lead and we haven't even left our pitch. Max, we'll figure out what happened for sure."

"Maybe, or maybe we already have our killer." I let my eyes drift to where we'd last seen Kelly, then turned back to Min.

Her eyes widened in surprise as she asked, "You mean Kelly? She couldn't have done it then come over and helped to figure out who we found, surely?"

"Maybe it's a ruse. Maybe she figured his identity would be discovered soon enough, so decided she may as well tell us. Stranger things have happened. Much stranger."

"I suppose it's possible. Not likely, but possible. She will have more control of the business, and she said it herself that Tina isn't as interested as her. Maybe you're right and it's a plot to take control and own everything outright."

"Or maybe it's the wife. If she's had enough of the pie business but Tim would never quit, it might be her way of finally putting an end to it. We have plenty to consider."

"We do. But we also need to unwind and have fun. It's awful, but we can't let it be the only thing we do this weekend. I want to enjoy myself too."

"And we will. I'm with you on that. We're here to have a break and that's what we'll do. Let the dust settle, look around, and see what turns up. There's no point trying to rush things, and without Tina here we can't sound her out anyway. I imagine she'll be back later today, or tomorrow at the latest, so let's leave it be until then and see what we can come up with without trying too hard. It sounds callous to say that, but I don't know what else we can do."

"It's not callous. We promised to help and we will, and the best way is to get involved with things and see what we hear, and see how everyone is acting. We're allowed to have fun."

With it settled, we decided to relax at the pitch for a while then check out the competition in an hour.

I milled about, antsy and unnerved by the madness and horror that yet again didn't feel quite real. It was as though I was living out a story, and felt disassociated from it in part, able to cope and deal with everything because somehow it was fake, or staged, or a waking dream. I knew from reading, and plenty of experience, that this wasn't unusual, and that many people involved in such things became remote and detached as a way of coping and making sense of this thing we called death.

Min was the same, and kept walking around, picking things up, staring at them, then putting them back down before staring off into the distance.

"We need to stop thinking about it," I said as we bumped into each other, literally, under the shade of the gazebo. "It's awful what happened, but life is for living and we deserve to enjoy ourselves. Let's forget about everything for a while and settle down and watch everyone have fun.

How about a drink? I have Prosecco. Lots of it." With a cheeky wink, I didn't even wait for an answer, and hurried over to the coolbox packed with ice from the supermarket and a selection of drinks.

"You read my mind," she laughed, grabbing a few glasses then setting out the small green folding table and placing it between the chairs.

Anxious came over for a quick inspection—there was always the chance of snacks—then huffed in disgust when I set the Prosecco down and glanced at us accusingly.

"Hey, we deserve it," I said. "We're on holiday, and are allowed to chill. It's been a crazy day so far, with way too much happening, so leave us to unwind without judging."

"And besides," added Min, "it's already past three. Wow, the day's gone so fast."

"It sure has." I sat, then poured the drinks, and we clinked glasses.

We sipped, both sighing, ignoring Anxious as he shook his head, trying to make us feel bad for our daytime drinking. He soon grew bored so retreated to the gazebo, having decided he wasn't going anywhere near Vee for the time being, as it still seemed too dangerous.

The booze went down nicely, if a little too fast, and neither of us were big drinkers normally, so after a top-up we sipped slowly and relaxed into our chairs as best we could—fifteen pound camping chairs were not ideal for slumping, but we did our best anyway! The day wore on, and we lost ourselves in our own little world of chatting about this and that, nothing deep or serious, and watching everyone enjoy themselves. The worries and drama of earlier were forgotten for a while, and we immersed ourselves in each other's company and the beautiful surroundings. It truly was a magical place and I vowed to return when there was nothing going on to wander around the grounds and take one of the trails.

The lake was the real draw, though, and I considered getting a blow-up paddle board as plenty of the places I stayed at had lakes for customers to use. Once again, the problem of space reared its ugly head, and I decided it wouldn't be worth the sacrifice I'd have to make with the rest of my gear, and was resigned to not always getting everything you wanted. Another life lesson vanlife had taught me.

The death slide was more popular than ever, with everyone having a go and screaming their way down the ridiculously vertical contraption. How long had it taken to build, I wondered, and what about safety concerns? It must have passed all the regulations, I supposed, but there was no way I was going on it again.

Visitors wandered past in a steady stream on their way to the stalls or to check out the campervans, chatting excitedly on their return about what they'd seen and the things they would like to implement in their own vehicles, or drooling over the pies they carried back to their pitches, keen for a mid-afternoon treat and maybe a few beers or glasses of wine to wash it all down. It was a true festival atmosphere, even without music, the buzz of the crowds contagious, and soon we were both relaxed and happy, getting a second wind thanks to the community atmosphere.

I was so sedate that I dozed off, only waking when Min shook me by the shoulder and whispered, "The giant pie competition is about to start. We don't want to miss what will surely be the highlight of the year." She gave me a cheery wink, then left me to wake up properly while she busied herself tidying away things. I turned and watched, grinning to myself, as I loved her dearly but she never used to be so fastidious about tidying up. Guess vanlife and the need for everything to be in its correct place had finally begun to rub off on her.

Taking a moment, I stretched out and yawned, noticing that the lake had gone quiet and nobody was on the death slide. A garbled announcement came over the tannoy, presumably declaring the competition was about to begin, so I hurriedly slipped on my Crocs, stood, stretched again, and went to help Min sort things out. I needn't have bothered as she had everything under control.

"What are you grinning at?" she asked as she slipped a bottle of water, Anxious' collapsible bowl, three apples, and a bag of crisps into her bag and slung it over her bare shoulder.

"Nothing. You look very pretty today. You've caught a little sun, and you're slimmer than ever."

"Oh, thank you." Min brushed gleaming hair from her face and smoothed down her pink vest, her skin glowing, legs strong and firm. As my eyes rose, so they met hers and she warned, "Stop ogling. That's rude."

"Sorry. It's just you look so fit and healthy. What's the secret?"

"Being a personal dietitian and knowing if I let myself go I'll lose some of my customers. Eating pies all day isn't helping, but I'm allowed to treat myself sometimes."

"Of course you are. We're on holiday. Come on, let's go and see who wins the competition. I wonder if Kelly will, or if someone else will beat them this year?"

"Let's hope she does win. The poor girl deserves it, and so does Tim's wife. What a horrendous day for them."

Anxious ran rings around us as we weren't moving as fast as he wanted, especially as Min had his lead in her hand, so we locked up after checking we hadn't left anything valuable out. The place felt safe, but it's always best to be sure. Then we headed along the dirt track past the stalls towards the marquee where the competition was to be held today and prizes would be handed out tomorrow for the pie rolling. It was also the beer tent and had seen plenty of action all day with people sheltering from the sun and relaxing. As we approached, the noise levels rose and people began to crowd around.

It was evident that nearly everyone at the site wanted to check out giant pies, their attitude rather tongue-in-cheek as this wasn't exactly gourmet awards night. We managed to squeeze inside and discovered there was more space than expected, although it was certainly full. The tables were set up in a U shape along the entire length of the side and rear walls, the bar at the other end, with the pies laid out expertly on the tables, the artisans standing proudly behind their creations with their individual banners or posters showcasing their names and contact details.

A photographer was already doing the rounds, snapping away at everything, and three judges were walking slowly from one table to the next, heads close, whispering about the various criteria each pie had to meet. After they'd prodded, poked, squatted to inspect, and discussed things, they each tasted the pie after cutting it with an oversized knife, before nodding solemnly to the contestants and moving on to the next.

A hush came over the onlookers as everyone got involved in things, keen to guess who would win, commenting in whispers on whose pie looked best, arguing good-naturedly about which one was the biggest. As the judges finished with the last pie, it was announced that everyone was now free to wander around and inspect them too. A cheer went up, then excited guests made a beeline for the tables, jostling for position, keen to be the first to offer unsolicited advice to the professionals, and possibly even get a free taster.

That wasn't going to happen; there was strictly no eating of the pies. Everyone was told they could buy as many regular sized ones as they wished from the stalls outside once the competition was over, and this obviously meant that whoever won would do incredible business later. I wondered how many they would sell, and what happened to the leftover pies that those who believed they were in with a chance would have made, only to be sorely disappointed.

Tensions were running high, the stallholders jittery and understandably nervous, not helped by the less than expert opinions of those wandering past, commenting on pastry colour, pie size, and bargaining for a sample. We waited for the rush to die down, then started at the first table, which was Kelly's as they won last year. We didn't stay long, just said the pie looked amazing, and was definitely the largest, and she seemed to be handling things remarkably well.

"Any problems with the others?" I asked.

"Just the usual. Everyone playing mind games and trying to freak the others out. Nothing I can't handle. They've been nice to me as they know I'm on my own now since everyone's heard about Tim. That doesn't mean they aren't rubbing their hands together as they want to win, but it is what it is." Kelly shrugged, then wiped her face with a cloth. "Mind you, this pair next to me," she confided, moving her head close to us, "are a different story. They came second last year. Pie in the Sky is the name, and they're a nasty pair. Will do anything to win. They even tried to nobble our cheese last year. Swapped out the Vintage Cheddar for inferior rubbish and thought we wouldn't notice. The year before that, they nicked our potatoes then tried to fob us off with cheapo ones that would never have worked. We found the sack under their van and Tim and Tina want ape on them. Since then they've settled down, but there's no love lost. Look at them!"

We turned to the table next to Kelly's and smiled at the couple glaring at us. They scowled, then put their heads together and the man said something which made them both giggle then look to us. Kelly's hackles were up and she growled under her breath before turning away and telling us, "I can't stand them. Competition is fine, and good, but they're like children rather than people in their fifties. They're always tittering and looking at us, like they know something we don't. Well, they won't be laughing when we win again."

"Think you will?" asked Min.

"Too right I do. The pie just needed a few more minutes after I came back from seeing you guys, and it turned out perfect. Part of the rules state it has to still be hot when the judges sample it, which means nobody can just bake it beforehand and get up to any trickery. We all have the same chance. Mind you, it's all down to how big an oven you can get, or some people make their own. We went that way and Tim had this huge beast of a thing made. We'll win." Nodding, she dealt with questions from people milling about so we moved along the row to the next table, Pie in the Sky emblazoned on a very professional banner behind them.

"Hi," I beamed. "Nice pie."

We looked down at the pie.

Then the grey-haired woman gasped, clutched her throat, and face-planted into her creation. I wiped pastry, cheese, and potato from my face as her husband screamed, "She's dead! Someone killed my wife. Murder!"

Chapter 9

Min reached for my hand and I squeezed it tightly as I turned to her and wiped off the worst of the splattered pie. The husband was dragging his wife from the mess of cheese and potato, the perfect pastry falling in large lumps around him. Anxious darted forward and filled his boots, oblivious to the death in his haste to nab free food.

"Get back here!" I hissed, disappointed in him as he should have picked up on the vibe and behaved.

The little guy reversed out, going "Beep, beep, beep," then sat and cocked his head, his stomach resting on the grass.

Min bent and told him, "That was very naughty. Someone might be dead. That's no way to behave."

Suitably chastised, he hung his head, then had a brainwave and lifted a paw and stared at us while he whined.

"No way is that gonna work," I explained, stifling a smile as now was not the time for mirth. As he lay down and groaned, I turned my attention to what was important, and edged around the table to help the man settle his wife in a chair. Her head lolled, her limbs were heavy as she was rather large and clearly liked to sample their wares, so it was awkward but we managed.

By now a crowd had formed, so Min joined us and together we arranged her so we could get a proper look.

"What happened?" Min asked the man.

"I don't know," he sobbed. "She was fine, then just fell into the pie. Is she really dead? She can't be. We have a competition to win." Kelly joined us, and he spun on her, face a mask of vitriol. "You. It was you! You wanted Tim out of the way so you could take over, and now you've killed my Nancy. Murderer! She's a killer! Someone arrest her."

"Jake, calm down. Why would I kill Nancy? And how dare you say I killed Tim? He was a great guy and I thought the world of him."

"Liar. You're a liar. We know all about you lot. Always arguing, always shouting. Never getting along. That dumb brother of his was always causing trouble, but you got rid of him, didn't you, because you wanted the business. Now look what you've done. Just because you knew we were going to win this year. You couldn't stand it, could you? Now Nancy's dead."

We turned back to the poor woman in the chair. I bent to check on her, then she shot upright, her face turned beetroot red, she coughed, and a large gobbet of pie shot from her mouth, hit the table, careened off, and landed beside Anxious. He took one look at it then batted it away. Guess he had his limits.

Everyone gasped, then laughed with nervous relief, but I wasn't so sure that everything was fine and this had just been a case of food getting stuck. She'd been unconscious and looked dead to me.

"Got anything to say now?" demanded Kelly, hands on hips, looking smug yet angry. "You better say sorry. That was a terrible accusation. You know I thought the world of Tim."

"Liar! And just shut up!" Kelly's rival bent and focused on his wife, asking if she was okay, and what happened. She said she wasn't sure, and one minute she was fine, the next she felt strange then collapsed.

"Are you sure you're alright, love?" asked Jake.

"I… I don't know. Um, actually, I think…" Nancy heaved from the chair, batted Jake away, took a step forward, and like a repeat of a bad joke once again simply keeled over and face-planted into the pie. Jake screamed. We rushed forward to pull her from the mushy mess, and got her into the chair once more.

We waited, but she didn't stir, and her colour had gone, leaving her like a waxwork dummy. I bent, felt for a pulse, but got nothing. I shook my head at Min, who tried, too, but was shoved aside by Jake in a panic as he shook Nancy and shouted at her to wake up.

The police and the two young paramedics arrived and the crowd parted, then they rushed forward and checked on her, their demeanour telling me everything I needed to know. After several minutes, and them doing all they could to try to revive her, they stood, turned to Jake, and told him that Nancy had passed.

Jake wailed and flung himself at Nancy, hugging her lifeless figure tightly, sobbing into her shoulder. Her head dropped forward, pie fell from her mouth. There was no sudden re-awakening this time; Nancy was gone for good.

We backed up to give Jake and the paramedics space, and bumped into the two young officers, Kim and Jim.

"Are you two alright?" I asked.

"We should be asking you both that. We heard about Mike Almond coming to see you. He was chatting with his brother afterwards, moaning about you trying to do his job. He wasn't happy with you saying it was a murder."

"He's not a nice man," said Min. "What about you two? What do you think?"

They exchanged a look, but Kim shook her head at Jim.

"What is it? Don't we deserve to know?" I asked.

Kim sighed, then checked we weren't being overheard before moving close and saying, "We thought it was suspicious, but there's nothing we can do. Frank and Mike are old-timers and close to retirement so want an easy life, but Mark's a nice bloke and isn't convinced about what Frank's brother said, but he let it go as he doesn't want to rock the boat. Frank couldn't care less and has always been like that. It doesn't matter what we think."

"And what about now? That's three deaths in one day. Surely now something will be done? Actually, we did find something out. I'm not sure if Kelly's had a chance to tell the DI or not, but we showed her a picture of the man under the campervan, and it turns out it was Tim's brother. They were estranged, but it's definitely him. He used to work for High Pies until they fired him, and nobody had seen him for a while. Then he turns up under our van and his brother dies, face planting into his pie like poor Nancy here. That can't be a coincidence, surely? He even had a business card for High Pies in his back pocket!"

"It's beyond belief if it is a coincidence," said Jim, nodding to Kim.

"So what do we do? Think they'll change their minds and open a proper investigation? Actually do something?"

We turned at a commotion, and I spied the two much more seasoned officers along with Mike Almond barging their way through the crowd, ordering people to step aside. None of them looked happy.

"I guess we're about to find out," sighed Kim, stepping out of the way as the men arrived.

"What's going on here?" demanded Frank, then nodded to his brother, the detective, before all three glared at us like it was our fault. "An explanation please," he growled.

I cleared my throat and asked, "Do you know that the man under our camper was Tim's brother? Did Kelly tell you?"

"She did. A real coincidence."

"It was," agreed his brother. The detective got right up in my face and said, "It was still death by misadventure. The fool was trying to sneak in for free, most likely to speak to his brother, and paid the price."

"That's right," agreed Frank. "Shame, but these things happen. It's good we know who he was, and we've informed the family of both deaths now, but it changes nothing."

"Are you serious!?" asked Min, puffing out her chest, squaring her shoulders, and standing her ground when the brothers confronted her, practically snarling. "Two brothers dead in mysterious circumstances, and you didn't care. Now this poor woman, Nancy, died just like Tim. Face down in a pie. That proves you both wrong." She turned to the nice older cop, Mark, and asked him, "What about you? What do you think? You can't just go along with what they say. You don't think this is another accident, do you?"

"It does seem unlikely," he admitted. He faced the others and said, "Guys, we need to have a re-think. Something's going on here. We need to investigate. Mark, you need to investigate. I know it's your case, but at least take a look. See what the deal is."

"Fine," huffed Mike. "But I want this place cleared out. You hear me?" he addressed Kim and Jim and told them, "Get everyone out apart from the deceased's husband. I want a word with him." He turned slowly to us, rubbing at his blotchy face, sweating profusely because of the heat in the tent and his weight, and hissed, "That includes you two. I don't want you interfering, and what I said earlier still stands. This is nothing to do with you. Whatever is going on, if anything, is not your concern. Do not get in my way." With a grunt, he shoved past us, knocking us both aside.

I was about to grab him and give him what for when Min pulled my arm back and said, "Leave him be. It's not worth it. Men like that won't listen to reason. He's a bully. A mean, rude, unkind bully. He should never have been allowed to be a detective."

Mike ignored her words, but his brother barked, "You can't say that about an officer of the law."

"I can say what I want. He's a terrible detective. And you aren't much better. You dismissed this because you couldn't be bothered. Just want an easy life and to retire. Your job's to protect everyone, not take it easy and let a murderer kill again. This is on you and your brother. You didn't even try to figure it out. It was us showing Tank's picture to Kelly that let us know who he was, which is something you should have done."

"She's right, Frank," said Mark, grabbing him as he began to lunge. "Cool it. We should have asked more questions and shown Tank's photo to everyone. It was lax. Don't deny it. It's high time you began to pull your weight again."

"You what!? I pull my weight. Decades I've been doing this job. I deserve to ease into retirement."

"Not when there's work to be done, you don't."

We left them bickering and trailed after everyone else as Kim and Jim shouted instructions to leave the marquee.

Outside was understandably chaotic, with people milling about, most of whom had no idea what had happened. Like quickfire, the news soon spread that another of the contestants had died, and the gossip began to build as the temperature rose. Groups of vendors speculated whether there was a pie maker serial killer on the loose, having immediately linked the two deaths and the fact they both died the same way. Visitors were confused, most not having heard about Tim, or Tank, but the moment they did a wave of panic spread through the crowd, many people shouting their concerns at the two bewildered young officers who were trying their best to ease everyone's concerns whilst ensuring nobody entered the marquee.

We bumped into Kelly as we tried to escape the melee, literally almost knocking her over as we backed away.

"Sorry. Are you alright?" I asked, taking her arm to steady her as she began to topple over backwards.

"I... I'm fine. At least, I think I am. What is going on around here? First Tim, then Tank, and now Nancy. Can't say I liked the woman, her and Jake are always trying to mess with our bakes, but that's no way to go. Just like Tim. Face in a pie. Awful." Her ponytail slapped around her shoulders as she shook her head rapidly as if to dispel the awful sight of Nancy. She rubbed at blotchy cheeks and blew her nose, her dark eyes closing as she took several deep breaths to calm her nerves.

"It doesn't sound like you got on with Nancy and Jake," noted Min with sympathy. "He said some harsh words about you and your business."

"He's always been like that. Nancy too. They tried to say we cheated last year, they were so put out, and will do anything to win. It was them who cheated, not us."

"How did they cheat?" I wondered.

"Pre-made the pie at their factory, or tried to, but the judges got wind of it and they had to start again from scratch here. Mind you, Nancy and Jake said that was just a trial run and they'd brought it with them for inspiration, but everyone knew they were going to try and use the pie as their entry. Big cheats."

"Jake said you were always arguing with Tim. Is that true?" asked Min, looking my way from the corner of her eye but discreetly. We were obviously both thinking the same thing.

"We had our moments. Who doesn't when they work together? But he was a real friend. Tina too. We're together constantly, work crazy hours, do the festivals, and it's just the three of us. We have to bake, serve, do the books, deal with suppliers, run the machines, cover the overheads, and everything a business entails. There's bound to be a few squabbles."

"Of course there are." I recalled some of the arguments I'd had with people I worked with over the years, and cringed at how I'd behaved and the things I'd got worked up about. I couldn't ever imagine going back to such a life, and was pleased to be well out of it.

"What should we do now?" I wondered.

"Let's get away from here. The competition is cancelled, I assume, so maybe we should go back to the van." Min smiled at me, nodding her head slightly at Kelly, then frowning. She wasn't sure about her now, was questioning if she might be involved, and although I had taken to her, I was having doubts too.

"Good idea," I agreed. "Kelly, what about you? What will you do now?"

"Wait here then pack up, I guess. What a nightmare. First Tim, now Nancy. They'll never do the competition and we won't get the business we expected. The whole next year is ruined. We'll be ruined." Kelly rubbed at her eyes, refusing to let the tears flow freely; she was a strong woman and wouldn't be beaten. Or was it something else, and she was merely lamenting that her plan hadn't worked as she wanted it to?

Maybe she'd done something to Nancy earlier and had expected to get rid of the competition before the judging began? I hated to doubt her like this, but knew from experience that anyone could be responsible and often it was the person you suspected the least or seemed like they had the most to lose.

We were itching to get away and discuss things, but just as we were about to leave a commotion erupted from the entrance and the onlookers shifted aside as the paramedics brought out Nancy on a stretcher, her body covered over with a white table cloth. Jake hurried along beside her, looking utterly distraught, his world having collapsed. His life would never be the same again. A lifetime of companionship was over, a business most likely finished, shared passions and so many memories now all that remained. I couldn't even imagine dealing with such a monumental upheaval and such a deep loss. Without Min, I didn't know what I would do or how I'd cope.

"They're moving her already?" gasped Min.

"That was quick. Surely they aren't calling this another accidental death?" I couldn't believe it. Even the DI had to have his suspicions now, surely?

As the older officers and Mike passed, I stepped in front of Mark, the only one I figured might be forthcoming, and stopped him while the others followed the paramedics. "What's going on? You're moving her already?"

"Not my call," he said gruffly, eyes on the retreating figures of his partner and the DI. He leaned in to me, the smell of coffee strong on his breath, and admitted, "It's not how I'd do things, but I'm just a copper, not the one running this shambles. Mike insists it was another death by natural causes, most likely brought on by the heat in the marquee and the excitement of the competition. Reckons the place is jinxed and that's why two people have died like that. The stress of it all, he said. Mind you, he also said they were idiots as who cared about how big a pie was? So, that's it. All done. An accident."

"But you don't think so? Mark, this is insane. Are we meant to go about our business like normal?"

"You are, yes. This isn't a case for you, Max. Leave it well alone. Mike has a real nasty streak, Frank, too, so leave it be. Enjoy the rest of your time here, but don't get involved. You'll regret it if you do."

"Was that a threat?" I asked, bristling.

Mark held his hands up to placate me and said, "No, I'm not threatening you. If it was down to me things would go differently, but I know Frank, worked with him for years unfortunately, and I know his brother. They're the same. Cops who don't care. It is what it is. They want an easy life as both are retiring soon, and Mike's never been one to be bothered if he solves a case or not. For him, this is just a few untimely deaths and that's the end of it. Leave it be. Everything will be back to normal soon, so that's the end of it." With an apologetic smile, he hurried off to catch up with the others.

Before I could tell Min what he'd said, the young officers called for everyone's attention. Looking very embarrassed, they explained that the competition could resume as although it was sad that Nancy had died, she'd want the event to continue.

"She bloody wouldn't," spat Kelly. "She'd hate to think it would carry on without them having a chance to win. She'll be spitting, wherever she is now."

"You don't want it to go ahead?" I asked, surprised.

"Course not! Some things are more important than money, and that's giving people dignity. She shouldn't have been moved so soon. They haven't even called it a crime scene. This isn't right. If I didn't know better, I'd day that either Mark, or Frank, or maybe both brothers are the ones behind this. Killing people and covering it up."

"What possible reason could there be for them doing that?" I asked, shocked.

Kelly turned to me, eyebrows raised, and asked, "Oh, didn't you know? They used to be in the pie game. Had a small business supplying local places with pies, and did all the competitions. They never won, though, and went bust eventually. Their pies were awful. They only ever made a go of it because of their local contacts, but eventually they went under." Kelly hurried off back into the marquee along with everyone else, leaving Min and I staring at each other with endless questions but no answers.

Chapter 10

With a shrug, and a promise that we would talk about what happened later, and that we'd definitely be opening another bottle of Prosecco, possibly two, we trailed in after everyone else and stood near the entrance where it was a little cooler. It had become stifling inside, and with the press of bodies now greater than ever thanks to the unforeseen drama, the heat and humidity were rising to dangerous levels.

I was astonished that things had returned to normal so rapidly, and I think everyone else was, too, especially the competitors and judges. Nevertheless, they'd been told by the authorities that they could continue, so that's what they did. Everyone took their places at the tables, the judges did their rounds again, this time sampling the still steaming pies, then retreated to a table in the corner where they sat and made notes, discussed the pies, and generally left everyone on tenterhooks.

Kelly was sweating buckets like all the others stuck at the tables, and I worried for her as she was bright red and looked ready to collapse. Seeing her like this, I felt bad for suspecting her, but then the thought crossed my mind that she might be stressed because of the risk of losing, not because she'd murdered three people. Was I a terrible person, or was it right to think this way?

I came out of my reverie as a hush descended over the marquee. The judges were on their feet and doing a final walk around the tables. They spoke in whispers as they went from table to table, but it seemed like it was a mere formality. After doing the rounds, they stood in the middle of the room then just like at crufts an elderly female judge in a smart blue suit and swept back silver hair marched forward and gave third place to a delighted pair of women in their thirties who whooped and fist-pumped the air before hugging.

Next came second place. The judge paused for dramatic effect before marching over to the vacant table of Nancy and Jake and pinned the rosette to the cloth.

Kelly let out a loud sigh and a nervous laugh, her eyes glued to the judge as she returned to her companions. They put their heads together momentarily, then the judge nodded and made a beeline not for Kelly but to the opposite side of the room. Kelly gasped, her head hung low, but her eyes followed the woman. Turning at the last moment, the judge smiled, then walked slowly around the room, clearly enjoying the heightened drama and sense of anticipation.

She paused at several tables, the poor people's eyes wide as they wondered if they'd won, but she kept on moving. With two strong strides, she marched over to Kelly, pointed at her, and handed over the first prize rosette.

Kelly whooped, held the rosette aloft, and promptly collapsed into her chair in relief, a broad grin on her flustered face.

"She seems relieved," noted Min with a wry smile.

"Sure does. I guess if it's her killing everyone, it wouldn't have made any difference to the outcome. Nancy died after the pie was on the table, so it had already been judged. If she wanted to ensure she won, surely she would have done it yesterday or earlier before they'd made them?"

"Maybe she tried, but it didn't work. You saw how Nancy reacted. She collapsed, then seemed fine for a moment, then died. Maybe it's a poison and she isn't sure how to use it properly."

"It's possible. What I'm really interested in is the news that the DI and his officer brother used to be pie makers too. That puts a whole new spin on things."

"Sure does. Come on, let's congratulate Kelly. We can discuss this later. What a day. I'm beat. Wish I'd had a nap earlier like you."

"You can have one in a bit if you want."

"You know I never sleep in the day." I raised an eyebrow and Min admitted, "Maybe now and then. But usually I'm just resting my eyes."

"Sure you are." I winked at her, took her hand, and together we followed after Anxious who had stayed close because of the upset but was now keen to see if any pies happened to "accidentally" fall off the tables. We hurried to catch up before he caused even more mayhem.

Once the well-wishers had spoken to Kelly, many offering little more than begrudging grunts or a quick, "Well done," before marching off, we approached the table and congratulated her. She was buzzing, but sweating badly, and seemed more stressed than ever.

"What's wrong? Aren't you happy?" asked Min.

"Yes, of course I'm delighted, but what if I'm next? Tim's gone, and his brother, and now Nancy. Does someone have it in for us?"

"The competition maybe?" I suggested.

"I don't know, and that's what makes this so awful. I wouldn't have been surprised to find out it was Nancy and Jake who'd done for Tim and Tank so they could win, but now it means it's someone else. I don't understand. What's the point? The pies were already made."

"That's what Max said. If it's to disrupt things, they should have acted earlier."

"I know, right? So dumb. Anyway, I'm absolutely beat, but I have to go and see to the stall. We're going to sell a ton of pies this afternoon and evening, and even more tomorrow when more people arrive. I've already had calls from our regular customers, and some new ones, so the phone will be going non-stop too. Oh, and Tina called. She said there was nothing she could do at the morgue, so she'll be back in a few minutes. She was so pleased we won, but distraught that Tim will never know."

"She's up for running the stall after her husband died?" I asked.

"She said she needs to keep busy. That there's nothing else she can do and Tim would want her to make the most of winning. I get it. She's put as much into the business as me, so doesn't want it to fail. Sorry, but I have to go."

We left her to gather her things and retreated to the entrance and the cool air blowing in, then headed outside and away from the people milling about, gossiping.

Our shoulders relaxed as we moved away from everyone, and Anxious perked up and skipped about, sniffing trails and wagging excitedly as people passed us by with pies. He tried the old poorly paw trick a few times and got a few treats until Min told him off for being a big naughty cheater. He looked sad for all of whatever the smallest measurement of time is then ran around merrily, enjoying the party atmosphere as people resumed risking their life on the death slide and splashed about in the water while others bought food or wandered around admiring the campervans on display.

"Oh boy, that's a relief," sighed Min as she sank into a chair and slipped off her sandals.

I retrieved the wine and glasses then sat beside her, took my Crocs off, stretched out, and closed my eyes as I lifted my head to the sun. "So good to be back home. Crowds are so stressful. There's no room to even breathe. It makes me appreciate the space here even more. Let's just drink some wine, and not talk about any of it for a while, okay?"

I turned to Min when she didn't answer, only to find her fast asleep with Anxious curled up in her lap, snoring already. With a chuckle, I grabbed my wine, sipped, and let the isolation wash over me. I began to relax, not even realising how tense I was until now.

It took longer than usual for me to settle. The busy morning, the deaths, the dealings with so many strangers, and then the press of bodies in the marquee had left me utterly drained yet hyped at the same time. Although I was definitely a people person, I wasn't somebody who did well with groups, preferring to be with just one or two others at a time. People sapped my energy rather than gave me more; I needed quiet time alone to recharge my personal batteries and to gather my thoughts and process things. Now I had it, and I welcomed the solitude.

Especially because the two souls I loved more than anything were right beside me, so I wasn't strictly alone. Vowing not to think about what had happened, I switched off and watched people with a detached eye, which was worrying, so I popped it back in and could see much more clearly! Chuckling to myself at my own private joke, I nevertheless did people watch without a thought in my head, observing them like I was from another planet and trying to understand the behaviour and strange rituals of this peculiar race of bipeds.

How odd the creatures were. They seemed to enjoy splashing around in water even though they didn't need to clean themselves, and the majority carried excess weight on their puny frames yet were always eating or drinking despite needing neither. Why was that? Most unusual and impossible to decipher was their obsession with making noise. It was non-stop. They spoke when they had nothing to say, and often in high-pitched tones that signified amusement even though there was nothing in their situation that was funny. And they also seemed rather obsessed, especially the younger generation, with risking their fragile lives by sliding down an obstacle built for no other reason than to terrify.

After pretending to be an alien, and finding it very amusing, I came back to my own thoughts and they began to grow dark so I had another glass of wine and refused to let it get to me. This was not my responsibility. It was nothing to do with me. I wasn't meant to solve this. The police were. Sure, over the last year I'd got involved in so many crimes and solved them, but surely there was a limit to how much a man should feel he had to figure out? Should I walk away? Ask Min if she'd leave with me and let this lie?

Being honest with myself, I knew that I couldn't do that. This was my destiny, and although I hated to admit it, it definitely made vanlife exciting. How could it not? Interspersed with quiet campsites, days, sometimes weeks staying beside stunning coastal spots, or in the middle of nowhere and exploring ancient castles or finding hidden waterfalls, hiking, sunning myself, trying to stay warm and dry, there was always that little thrill that surfaced, wondering if something would happen and I could help.

Now was the time to step up, and not take it personally that the very odd DI, Mike Almond, or his just as unhelpful brother, Frank, seemingly didn't care at all. I owed it to the families to do what I could, but I also owed it to myself, to Min, and yes, to Vee. It felt personal because of Tank, and I got the sneaking suspicion that my beloved Vee would not be a happy campervan if I let this one slide. No way was she going down for murder, not on my watch.

As the intense heat of the day faded, people gradually left the lake to get into dry and warm clothes, and the site grew quieter as everyone retreated to tents or vans, or left after a fun day out. I gathered wood I had stored in Vee and got out the small portable fire bowl I'd got for a steal off Amazon, and busied myself doing man stuff, the primordial lure of fire consuming me. A simple task, but one that had its own set of rituals, and something I could never tire of. I lit the fire first time, always nice for a smug sense of a small win, then added tiny slithers of kindling and gradually built it up in a perfect pyramid to retain the heat inside and give every piece the same chance to burn brightly.

Once satisfied, I scooted over in my chair and sat next to it, the warmth not really needed but a comfort nevertheless. With Min and Anxious still asleep, I stared into the flames and finally turned my attention to the most important matter of the day. What to make for dinner! We had several options, including pies, but I figured they would do for a picnic lunch tomorrow. After mulling it over and going through a mental checklist of what I had in the tiny fridge and coolbox, I came up with a simple but tasty dish that I was surprised to discover when I thought back I hadn't cooked for ages. Beef stew. An oldie, but definitely a goodie. Packed with flavour, very filling, comforting, and also very easy and quick to prepare.

To some it would sound silly, but I was excited with my decision and couldn't wait to get started. Cooking was something familiar, something I excelled at. I wasn't being big-headed; it was just a fact. It was also something I knew brought joy to others. Min loved it when I cooked now, the one-pot vow I'd made meaning I refrained from overthinking meals or taking too long preparing and faffing about, so I didn't get lost in my cooking, rather got about the business of what needed to be done, then let it do its own thing for the most part.

Whistling, and happy, I peeled, sliced, chopped, boiled, seared, smiled smugly, swished my fancy knives around as nobody was looking, and had several more sips of wine, giggling as the pot came to a boil as I knew that now I had nothing to do for several hours but sit, drink, and wait for dinner which should be ready at about seven just as it began to cool down properly. With the fire blazing, I sat and stared into the flames after I'd cleared up the mess in the kitchen, and there I remained until Min and Anxious woke twenty minutes later, both looking confused for a moment until they remembered where they were. Min smiled at me, Anxious yawned and did likewise, and my heart sang for joy.

"Evening, sleepyheads. Usually it's me waking up from a nap, but this time you're the ones who missed all the action."

In a panic, Min asked, "What did I miss?" and looked around for signs of something exciting.

"Just teasing. Nothing happened at all. It's been awesome. Glass of wine?"

"Oh, yes please. What a lovely nap. I really needed it. It's been such a whirlwind of a day." Min came over to me cradling Anxious, then they both kissed my cheek. One kiss was much wetter than the other.

I sorted out a drink for Min and fresh water for Anxious and they both drank greedily until their thirst was quenched. "Another? I asked them both with a raised eyebrow. They held out bowl and glass so I topped them both up then sat next to them and sighed happily. "What a day. Crazy, eh?"

"Sure was. At least now we can relax."

"You've been doing that for at least an hour, if not longer," I laughed.

"I needed a quick nap," she said, giggling. They both sniffed and turned to me. "Is that dinner I smell?"

"Beef stew. It'll be ready in a few hours, so we have plenty of time to soak up the atmosphere and relax."

"Oh, wow. Great. I don't want anything crazy to happen. I want to sit, drink, eat, chat with you guys, and not have anything to do but chill out."

"Apparently, you can't say chill out any more."

"What? Why not?"

"The kids just say chill." I shrugged, but I'd heard it from the twins on my last murder mystery adventure, and they'd set me straight. "Apparently, it's old-fashioned and makes you seem like a total oldie. You can't say chilling either. It's chill."

"Then I shall chill." Min smiled at me and I felt the love radiate. What a woman!

We sat and chatted about this and that, avoiding anything serious, just easy banter and a slight feeling of the booze hitting, but we paced ourselves and mostly just stared at the fire as the sun sank lower. There were still hours of daylight left, however, and after a while we decided a walk would be nice to see what the site looked like and to give Anxious a bit of a run around.

I checked on dinner, gave it a stir, then added a few pieces of wood to the fire so it would be going nicely when we returned. After locking up, we headed along the path, holding hands and talking quietly. The air felt magical as this truly was a special place, and everyone we passed smiled and said hello, people seemingly in good spirits and enjoying the chance to relax too.

Then we bumped into the two young officers, Kim and Jim. Kim was crying, Jim looked furious, and both were looking like they wanted to whack someone with their truncheons.

"Problem?" I asked.

Chapter 11

Jim turned his head, still cradling Kim, her cheek pressed against his bony shoulder, and managed a half smile. It was clear he was fuming and upset, but he tried to straighten up and look official. Kim stirred from his embrace and stepped back, then wiped her eyes hurriedly and pulled her hat low over her face to try and hide her upset.

"Sorry, just having a moment," said Jim.

"I must look a right mess," Kim laughed weakly, tugging at her jacket and teasing wayward curls from her face before plastering on a very fake smile.

"You look fine," said Min. "What's the matter? Why're you standing here like this? Has something happened?"

Both looked around to see who was about, but we were on our own at the end of the stalls beside their gazebo with nobody else near. Most people were at their pitches now, relaxing and eating, enjoying the early evening.

"If we tell you, do you promise to keep it to yourselves?" asked Jim, tugging at his crisp, white shirt collar.

"Of course," I agreed.

"We know who you are, heard people talking, especially Mark and Frank, so we looked you up, Max. You, too, Min. And wow, you guys get about. Max, you're an internet sensation, you know? A true legend."

"Tell me about it," I sighed, wishing it wasn't so. "But what's that got to do with why you're both so upset?"

"Because you might be our last hope," said Kim, checking with Jim that it was okay to say it. He nodded his agreement.

"For what?" I knew what was coming, but had to be sure we were on the same page.

"To help solve this. Mike Almond insists the deaths were accidents, and won't hear of us looking into things. Told us to stay away or our time on the force would be short."

"He can't do that, can he?" asked Min.

"He can," said Jim. "He's one of the old crowd and knows everyone. Can put in a word and ensure that our lives are made so miserable that we'll have no choice but to quit. I don't want to do that! We both worked so hard to get onto the force, and now it might be ruined."

"His brother's just as bad," said Jim, taking up the story. "He told us to mind our own business and not to ask questions or make fools of them. Said to leave this alone and they know what they're doing. We tried to get his partner, Mark, to make them see sense, but he won't do anything. Mark's a nice guy, but is retiring soon, too, like the brothers, and doesn't want to rock the boat. We just had a massive argument with all three of them, and it got heated. Mike had the final word and warned us not to interfere or else."

"Why are they so against anyone asking a few questions?" I wondered.

"Because they're lazy, fat slobs itching to retire and don't want to have to do the paperwork or the legwork. Mike Almond is grossly overweight and should have been made to retire years ago, not that he should ever have been a detective in the first place. It's about who you know, and he knows everyone."

Jim put a hand to Kim's shoulder as she hyperventilated and said, "It's okay. Don't get so upset. It isn't our fault."

"I know that! Sorry, I'm not angry with you. It's just..." Kim put her hand over Jim's and smiled at him. They were clearly close.

Jim looked us both in the eye, face solemn, and said, "The fact is, none of them want to do anything. This is an easy gig for Frank and Mark, and they're just seeing out their time. When Mike got called in to be the lead detective, they were both pleased as they knew he'd take the easy option if possible. That's what he's done."

"But are you saying that Mike really doesn't care if it was a murder?" I asked. "Surely if he thinks there's a killer on the loose he'd investigate? He can't be that bad."

"It's not that he's trying to cover anything up," said Kim, regaining her composure, "it's that he won't bother to think or search for clues or treat it like it's murder. We heard it was you and Kelly who discovered the identity of the man under your van, and that shouldn't have happened. We should have been allowed to show photos to people involved, and then we would have found that out. He should have been more pro-active."

"And now we've been warned off this," hissed Kim, her fists clenched.

"Did you know that both Mike and his brother used to be pie makers?" asked Min. "They had a business like the others here, but it went bust a few years ago. Apparently, the pies weren't that great and they never won any prizes, and the business caved. That means they most likely know the people here, or know of them."

"You what!?" growled Jim.

"You're serious?" asked Kim, shaking her head.

"We are." Min drew me towards the pair and with our heads close she asked, "So what do we think? Could they possibly be involved? I mean, like they're out for revenge or something? Who knows what happened to make their business go under, but what if it was to do with someone here, or they just can't stand to be out of the picture and want to get back at everyone who's successful?"

"That's the first we've heard of this, but we're new to the force and only a few months out of training. Sure, there are plenty of stories about Mike and Frank, not so much about Mark as he seems like a nice guy, but nobody ever mentioned that. Guess it was before all the new cops' time. We were warned about them by some of the older crowd, but nobody mentioned a side business."

"Then maybe it's nothing," I said. "But it's certainly a crazy coincidence. Could they be involved?"

"You mean murder? No way," insisted Jim. "They might be lazy and disinterested, but kill members of the public? I can't see them going that far. And besides, it would take too much effort. They're too lazy to bother." Jim laughed, and turned to Kim for her opinion, but she just gnawed at her knuckles, eyes unfocused. "Kim, you don't think they had anything to do with this, do you?"

"No," she sighed. "I don't like them, but no, they aren't killers."

"It would be a stretch," I agreed, "but we thought it best to mention it. Sorry you've had such a bad day. What will you do now?"

"What we're told. Which means nothing much. We'll keep an eye on things, and do what we can to ensure nobody else gets killed, but without any clues and orders to stay out of it, we'll just wander around and show ourselves."

"I don't think there will be any more killings anyway," I said, convinced of it. "Whatever this is about is done now, and whoever is responsible will be feeling very pleased with the result. Maybe they timed it to happen here exactly because they knew who would be running the investigation. That's something to think about."

"That's a good idea!" said Kim, smiling at me. "Jim, he's right. I bet the killer knew this place was perfect to do what they did as the chances were high they could walk away scot free."

"It's the right place to commit murder if you don't want anyone trying too hard to solve the crime," agreed Jim. "Thanks, guys. We knew it was the right decision to talk to you. We're going to be discreet, but ask around anyway, and if we uncover anything, we'll be sure to let you know. We can't risk our futures, but we don't want this to go unsolved. We're convinced it was murder, so if nobody else takes this seriously then hopefully at least we can help you solve it."

"Whoa! We aren't saying we'll solve this," I insisted. "Look into things tomorrow, yes, but it might lead to nothing."

"That's all we ask. We'll do the same. We're off our shift soon, but are back tomorrow, and to see everything goes smoothly on Sunday when everyone leaves, so we'll see you then?" asked Kim.

We agreed we'd talk more tomorrow, so left them and continued our walk, with Anxious itching to run around after waiting so patiently for us to finish talking. As we were right by the open fields of the estate, we told Anxious he could go and play so he tore off, grateful to be able to burn off some of the excess energy that he always had in abundance.

Min and I linked arms and trailed in his miniature slipstream, laughing and pointing at his antics. A few minutes into the walk, I paused, and as Min turned I took her hands, looked into her eyes, and said, "I love you."

"Where did that come from?"

"I know you know that it's true, but I wanted to say it anyway. No reason, just that I do. It's not something we always say, and I know it's been a tough, stressful few years. Before you tell me off, I'm not going to start asking about the future, or dwelling on the past, none of that. Just know that I love you. Forget all the madness we seem to get involved in, the crazy stuff, all of it, because you are the most important thing in my life. Whatever the future holds, I will always love you."

"Oh, Max, you big, soppy idiot. I love you too."

"I know things haven't worked out how we might have wanted, but seeing Anxious running around, us walking arm in arm, it got me to thinking about what life might have been like if…"

"If we had children?"

"Yes. Sorry, I know I shouldn't have brought it up."

"No, I'm glad you did. We don't talk about it much, and that's fine, but it's good that you think about it sometimes."

"Do you? Think about it much, I mean?"

"Probably more than I should. Sometimes I feel sad, but other times I give myself a stern talking to and tell myself that I'm a very lucky woman. I live in an amazing country, I have my health, there's more money than I really need, I have a job, but most importantly of all I have you back. My man. My Max. It was so lonely for me for years as you sank further into your work obsession. I felt so isolated and like you didn't care about me. I know that isn't true, that you always cared, but it was hard. I'm sorry I made us get a divorce, but I didn't know what else to do."

"You did the right thing. I was awful," I chuckled. "Looking back on it now, I can't even believe it was me. I got lost back there for a few years, became something I can't stand, and I am truly sorry. Do you forgive me?"

"I do. For a long time I didn't, but after you saw sense and changed, became my old Max again, I was so happy for you. You're a fine man, Max Effort. The best."

We kissed, our closeness enveloping us like no words ever could, and I was the happiest man alive. Laughing at each other as we stood there, tongues licking our lips and the evening sun still strong, we turned and watched it sink below the trees at the edge of the field, the majestic, dark silhouettes crisp and so beautiful it made me want to weep. Or maybe that was because of the love I had from the most caring and beautiful woman in the whole world.

Huddling together just because we could, and wanting to feel the closeness, we continued our stroll, playing games with Anxious, running around, hiding behind trees, racing him across the field, and generally trying to wear ourselves out and forget about the madness raging back at the site and in the dark heart of whoever was responsible for taking three lives today.

I felt like a kid again, and lost myself in the joy of playing, of feeling my heart beating fast, legs aching, arms pumping, a massive grin on my face. Min needed this, too, and raced around like she was in training for a marathon, throwing in the occasional sprint, cajoling and teasing me to speed up as she and Anxious pelted past, breathing heavily.

We skipped, jogged, ran backwards, threw sticks for the little guy, and hid behind more trees, then jumped out and shouted, "Boo!" to a startled Anxious who howled his head off then ran off and hid behind another tree. He poked his head out to see if we were coming while we pretended to search for him and he barked happily, not connecting that we could hear him.

This was what it would be like to have a child, and I had to push the thought down and focus on the here and now and not lament what might have been. We had enough, more than enough, and much more than so many people in the world, so had absolutely nothing to complain about. The evening was perfect, and we had a wonderful life; I would not feel sorry for us.

We stopped for a breather, bent over and panting, while Anxious barked at us to go and hide again.

"He's unstoppable," laughed Min, her cheeks rosy, her eyes blazing with the buzz of the games and a raw happiness it's impossible to explain. Something deep down inside sparked by feeling truly free and living in the moment, doing something just because it's fun and for no other reason.

"He sure is. Let's play one more game, then get back to the pitch and have dinner. I've certainly built up an appetite."

"Me too. I'm famished. Okay, we'll hide, you come and find us. Count to thirty. I have a great place and you'll never find us."

"Right you are," I giggled, turning my back and beginning to count.

Anxious barked like he always did once someone began counting as he knew the fun was about to start. Min called him and he went silent as they snuck off to hide, while I continued to slowly count.

"Coming, ready or not," I called out, then turned, grinning and happy, and scoured the landscape for my quarry. I had to stifle a giggle and a shout of, "Found you," when I spotted Min's bum sticking out from behind a tree and Anxious' head at ground level, his paws over his eyes like that meant I couldn't see him.

I played along and ran over to a different small copse and made a big deal of jumping out around the sides of the trees as if I thought they were there. With Min giggling and Anxious barking, making it obvious where they were, but this was for Anxious as much as us, so I continued to make my way over, walking around each tree as I went, until I neared.

"Where can they be?" I shouted. "They're so good at hiding. I wonder if a biscuit will help me find them. Maybe if I wave it around like this, it might somehow point in the right direction and I'll win." Stifling a laugh, I did exactly that and Anxious barked then darted from his hiding place and headed straight for me.

"Hey, no fair!" shouted Min, shaking her fist at me but smiling.

"All's fair when it comes to hide and seek," I insisted, face serious, then burst out laughing as Anxious skidded to a stop in front of me and sat, eyes locked on the biscuit, and barked once.

I bent and gave him his treat, then turned sharply when Min let out a cry.

"Are you alright?"

"Just tripped on something. I hurt my ankle."

"Don't move. Wait for me." I hurried over with Anxious on my heels, his treat already devoured. Min was sitting with her legs out, rubbing at her ankle, surrounded by young trees in a mossy area where stumps had begun to rot, clearly felled then new saplings planted. I bent and asked, "Do you think it's broken?"

"No, it's fine. Just a slight sprain. I'll be okay in a minute. I just tripped back there." She pointed behind her at something sticking out of the ground, covered in moss. "Must have been a root or one of the stumps. It's lovely here, but hard to see what's underfoot."

I glanced over, then back to Min, but something was telling me to look again, so I walked over and bent at the protruding object and gasped.

"What is it?" Min called out.

"Looks like a bag. You tripped on the strap. It's one of those old military satchels similar to the one I have. This one's black, not green like mine, and a load of moss has been dumped on it."

"Wait for me! Don't you dare look at it until I'm there."

"Can you walk? Let me come and help." I rushed back, helped her stand, and Min tested out her ankle which she assured me was fine. She walked slowly over with me, shaking out her leg a few times, and then we stopped and looked down at the partially hidden canvas bag.

"We've found our first proper clue," she said, grinning.

"Sure looks that way," I agreed, matching her grin and raising an eyebrow. "Best to take it slowly and look around before we uncover it properly."

"Bit late for that," she smirked.

I groaned as I looked down to find Anxious digging in a frenzy with his front paws and kicking away the dirt with his hind legs, the bag already uncovered, the straps thankfully secured so he hadn't messed up whatever was inside.

We squatted, I grabbed Anxious, and together the three of us stared at the satchel.

Chapter 12

"Should we open it?" asked Min, a wicked twinkle in her eyes.

"The correct thing to do is alert the authorities."

"It is."

"But, unless it's a confession, and a signed one, and with fingerprints, you can bet that the DI will find a way to bury it as irrelevant."

"So, what you're saying is that it's our public duty as concerned citizens to open the bag and check if it's relevant to our case?"

"Our case?" I asked, eyebrows raised, smirking despite myself.

"Yes, Max, our case. Those poor young officers deserve a break, and to be proved right, not to mention Kelly and how upset she is."

"As long as she isn't the killer," I reminded her.

"Don't be daft! She's lovely. We should check what's inside."

"What do you think, Anxious?"

He raised a muddy paw, cocked his head, and licked his own nose.

"See, he thinks we should do it too," said Min.

"Since when does a nose lick mean open a bag that might contain evidence vital to solving a triple murder?" I asked, my eyebrows now making a break for it around the back of my head.

"Just open the bag!"

Carefully, I undid the two front buckles, then flipped over the straps and opened out the bag. I wasn't sure what I'd expected to find, money maybe, drugs, a stash of rare pies, but what we did uncover left us gasping. After we'd recovered, I pulled out a nasty looking gun, mindful to keep it pointed down, using the tips of my fingers wrapped in leaves so I wouldn't get fingerprints on it. I laid it aside, neither of us having spoken, and cautiously removed the only other item. A sealed ziplock bag that I didn't open contained five gold rings, a ten pence piece, a Zippo lighter with decorative scrolls etched into it, and a belt buckle that to my eye looked like it might have actually been either solid silver or at least silver-plated.

"Don't open the bag," warned Min.

"I wasn't going to. I don't want to get my fingerprints on any of this lot. Min, it's a real gun. At least I think it is." I picked it up again, the matte black metal menacing and surprisingly heavy. The grip was rough, with a series of ridges there to give you a firm hold, and to me it looked like you slid a magazine in the bottom then pulled back the front to prime it, but I didn't know anything about guns or the terminology, only that they were beyond dangerous and about as illegal a weapon as you could get in this country. Absolutely nobody was allowed to own a gun like this, I was sure, and you'd be facing prison just for getting caught with it.

"What do the rings mean? And a ten pence piece is odd. Plus a belt buckle. Even a lighter. That's a weird collection of things."

"Maybe they're all worth money. The rings would be, the buckle, too, if it's antique and solid silver. Maybe the ten pence is a rare one and the Zippo might be silver as well. I can't tell."

"And someone buried it out here? What for?"

"To pick up later, I guess, or possibly it was left as payment to someone and they would come and collect at some point."

"Think it's tied to the murder?" Min laughed the moment she asked, and added, "Sorry, of course it is. It has to be, doesn't it?"

"I would assume so."

"Let's have a little think about this and see what we can come up with. But, um, can you do something about the gun? It's freaking me right out. A real gun! Have you ever held one before?"

"I don't think so."

"You don't think so!? Surely you'd know. I know I haven't."

"Then no, I have never wielded a terrifying looking, heavy, clearly very expensive and beyond illegal gun."

"Then don't start," she laughed.

"I won't. What do you think it means? How does it relate to the killings?"

"No idea, but like I said, we need to have a think about this. Let's sit for a while and mull it over."

For a few minutes, we merely stared at the items. Once we'd finished, we both shook our heads. We'd come up with nothing. Were any of the deceased coin collectors or jewellery fans? Possibly smokers? Even if they were smokers, were they missing a Zippo lighter? And the reality was that even if that was the case, none of this gave us any idea who'd put it here or who it belonged to.

"We should tell the two youngsters," said Min.

"I think you're right. That way, we know it will be in the right hands, and not shoved in a drawer somewhere. But will it get them into trouble? If we tell them, they'll have to decide what to do with it. Maybe it puts them in an awkward position."

"That's for them to decide. They have their whole futures as cops ahead of them and if they want to be good ones, do their job properly, then they'll have to stand up to the likes of Mike and Frank and do what they're paid to do."

"Wow, that's pretty harsh."

"Maybe, or maybe not. Max, they're the law, just like the old guys, and nobody seems to be doing their job properly. Let's go and find them."

Min's ankle was fine, just a little tight when she began walking, but it eased off as we made our way back across the field. We found Kim and Jim returning from a patrol around the site, so explained what we'd found, their eyes widening at the mention of a gun.

"You didn't touch it, did you?" asked Jim, looking at me dubiously.

"Only carefully," I admitted.

"Max, that's dangerous, not to mention tampering with evidence," scolded Kim.

"I did not tamper. I handled carefully. With leaves."

"Oh, I'm so sorry, your lordship. I didn't realise you'd used safety leaves. Of course, how silly of me. Let me just get my own leaves, rather than my latex gloves, so I can be sure not to contaminate the evidence. Jim, do you know where our collection of police leaves are?"

"Are you being sarcastic?" I laughed, but also feeling bad. "I'm sorry I picked up the gun, but honestly, they were very thick leaves." I winked and Jim and Kim laughed.

"Sorry, Max, I was being harsh on you, but you should know better. I don't mean about fingerprints, the leaves were actually a good idea, but I mean handling a deadly weapon. By the sounds of it, that's a Glock, and if it had gone off it would have killed you. You better show us where it is. Why come to us?"

"Because we know you'll do the right thing with it," said Min. "We figured if we told Mike he might just dismiss it, but you two won't, will you?"

"We'll see it gets to the right people," said Jim, face determined, nodding at Kim. "This has gone on long enough with people like Mike and Frank. We can't let them push us around and bully us anymore. There's something weird going on around here, we're sure of it, so are you, and we won't hand this over to him. We'll tell our boss. He isn't a fan of them either, so will make sure they get their feathers ruffled and actually do something about the murders."

"Maybe, or maybe not," said Kim, "but either way, at least it will give us the chance to explain about what's been really going on around here and give our side of the story."

"I hope you don't get into too much trouble," I said.

"If we do, we do, but we haven't done anything wrong. We might be young, but that doesn't mean we're stupid. Lead the way." Jim marched off without waiting, then turned and I pointed in the other direction. "Um, ignore that last bit," he chuckled, looking embarrassed. "We may do the occasional stupid thing."

We showed them where the satchel was and they both took photographs. Then Jim called it in on his phone, speaking directly to his boss. He wandered off as the conversation continued, and returned a few minutes later looking jubilant but a little afraid too.

"What did he say?" asked Kim, repeatedly taking her hat off then putting it back on and playing with her hair.

"That he's sending a team! He said to touch nothing, that everything would be photographed and checked, and we were to start asking questions about everything that has gone on around here. He'd heard about the deaths, and had his suspicions that it wasn't being handled well, and had already spoken to Mike, Frank, and Mark about it. Apparently, they were ordered to perform a thorough investigation, and he's fast-tracked the autopsies to see if that uncovers anything. Should be done by the morning. Ugh, tomorrow will be a nightmare. They'll be so annoyed to have to treat this like a proper murder case, and with the gun it means it's been escalated so everyone will be watching how they handle things. Our lives are about to get difficult."

"You two can handle it," I said. "You seem like you're going to be great cops. I mean, you are already, of course, but you're handling this well and have the right attitude. Sorry, that sounds so trite and like I'm the expert, which isn't the case. What I mean to say is, um…"

"Max, it's okay, we get it," laughed Kim. "We were talking while we did our rounds, and after speaking with you guys we felt so bad. Like we were letting people down. It isn't how the police should act and we shouldn't let ourselves get bullied like we have, even if it means risking our jobs. If cops don't stand up to bullies, how do we expect others to do the right thing? No, we get it, and we're grateful for your faith in us after we pretty much told you that there was nothing we could do. There was, and is, and now we've done something about it thanks to you two."

"We do appreciate it so much," agreed Kim. You two head off and have your dinner. We can handle things from here. Enjoy your evening and we'll see you both tomorrow."

"You're sure?"

"Absolutely," said Jim. "Have fun, maybe some drinks, enjoy the warm evening and take it easy. We'll deal with the teams, and trust me, there will be a load of top brass along too."

With a nod, we left the two nervous young officers to it. They were excited, but clearly apprehensive, and I didn't blame them. They were about to stand up to two long-standing stalwarts of the police and had defied their orders to stay away from the deaths and not ask questions. What their future held was still in doubt, but at least they stood by their moral code and for what was right.

We were exhausted by the time we made it back to our pitch, but as we arrived the smell of the beef stew perked us up and we hurried over, taking a deep snort when I lifted the lid. It looked perfect, and was ready, so we washed up, sorted crockery, cutlery, and drinks, then I ladled some out for Anxious along with his dry food and then served ours. We sat on the blanket and tucked in, ripping off chunks of crusty bread with our hands and dunking it in the unctuous gravy and eating greedily.

The rich, dark stew was exactly what we needed. We hadn't realised how hungry we were until we began eating, but once we did we couldn't stop. The stress, and yes, the excitement, had given us both a raging appetite, and both had a second helping then a small third ladle and mopped up the still steaming gravy with the crusty bread until we finally had to stop as our stomachs became uncomfortable.

"That," Min placed her perfectly clean bowl down beside her, "was absolutely incredible! Max, how do you do it? I should be used to your cooking by now, but I still can't believe you make everything taste so absolutely amazing. Thank you. You always do the cooking and I feel like I'm not pulling my weight sometimes, but wow, I could never make something that tasty."

"Where did that come from? It's just stew!" I laughed, unable to hide my smile. "Thank you for the compliment. It's always nice to hear."

"I probably don't say it enough, but I do appreciate it."

"Min, you know I love cooking, and I especially enjoy cooking for you. I know you appreciate it. You don't have to say it."

"I wanted to, so you know I'm not taking it for granted. Not taking you for granted. Max, you've worked so hard to create a new life for yourself. I'm jealous, if truth be told."

"Of me?" I was surprised.

"Yes, of you. Is that such a shock?"

"Kind of. Considering what I put you through. What I put us both through. And Anxious. All the upset, the utter turmoil it caused. I know I've changed, and sorted things out, but I didn't know you were jealous. All I've done is what I should have been like anyway. I went off the rails."

"You did, but it wasn't only your fault. I should have done something."

"There was nothing you could have done. Let's face it, you tried, but I wasn't in the right place to listen. Too consumed with things that didn't matter, not really. Min, is everything alright? This isn't like you."

"Yes, everything's fine. Sorry, I'm just being silly. I suppose it's being here with you guys, and the weather getting nice again. I miss being with you both, and living like this. Being outside, seeing different places, having adventures."

"And murders," I reminded her.

"How could I forget?" she giggled, then turned serious as she shifted on the blanket, averting her eyes.

"What's really going on? You know you can tell me anything."

"I know. The honest answer is that I suppose I'm scared."

"Of what?"

Min turned back to me, her eyes welling with tears she brushed away then held my gaze and answered truthfully. "The future. Us. What will happen. How it might or might not work. What I'll do. My job, the house, the way you live. All of it. It's terrifying. Max, I know we promised not to talk about any of it until the year was up, until you've had a year living like this, and I've had the time to think and to see how you cope, how I cope, and to prove I can take care of myself alone, can manage, deal with everything, but it's been so hard and I just don't know what to do. It's already been life-changing since we split up, a massive upheaval, a totally different way of living being alone, and I'm scared of what the future might bring. I don't know what to do!"

"Hey, it's okay. Come here." I scooted over, put my arm around her, and she buried her face in my chest and cried softly. "I'm so sorry, Min. Truly I am. For everything. I know it's been so hard, and I regret it every single day. Don't be scared. You're a strong, capable woman and you've coped so well with everything that has happened. Whatever you decide, I'll agree to. You know what I want, but I understand it's a massive life choice. The biggest. Yes, it's terrifying, especially for you as you've spent so long rebuilding a life for yourself, so I get it. You'll make the right choice as whatever it ends up being, it's the one you know will be best for you."

"For us, Max. It has to be the correct choice for both of us. Gosh, why does life have to be so complicated?"

"If it wasn't a challenge, it wouldn't be worth fighting for. And know this, Min Effort. I will never stop fighting for you. For us."

"I know. That's what makes it so hard." Min pulled away and wiped her tears, then smiled bravely at me. "I'm so silly. A fool. Look at me blubbing away and acting like I'm the most important thing in the world when people are dead. Murdered. It puts it into perspective."

"You are the most important thing in the world," I told her, meaning it.

We sat there in silence for a while, lost in each other's eyes, and gradually the sadness faded and we began to smile. Then we laughed. We laughed at the absurdity of it all. Here we were, two people who loved each other dearly, torn apart then coming back together because of the deep bond we had, yet why did it always end up being so complicated?

Because that's what life was. One messed up, complicated, impossible to decipher quagmire you had to fight your way through, making decisions on the fly and hoping they were the right ones. Battling for happiness, and hoping you didn't ruin it.

This time, I would not ruin it. This time, I would do whatever it took to ensure Min was happy. I just prayed that meant with me and Anxious.

Chapter 13

After our serious talk and the ensuing laughter at the absurdity of it all, we agreed on several points. We were taking things way too seriously and had absolutely nothing to complain about. Whatever the future held, we would always have each other. Currently, Min and I were both in fine health and had zero money worries, which we were both beyond grateful for. After ticking off these important points, we found ourselves in extremely good spirits.

We played a few games of Exploding Kittens with Anxious, his new favourite game for obvious reasons, then he skipped off over to Vee and settled on the bed after I pulled it out and arranged things, cosying on down with the latest incarnation of Sir Snugglington. Min and I eased into our chairs with a nice glass of wine once the kitchen was sorted and I'd given everything a final wipe down for the evening.

There was no talk about the murders as we'd run out of things to say, and speculation was getting us nowhere, so we avoided the topic and kept the mood light, not wanting to spoil it. People passed our pitch, out for an evening stroll, soaking up the festival atmosphere, the whole site buzzing despite there being no music or anything to actually see or do after the fun in the lake and the competition earlier. Obviously, news had spread about the deaths, but the focus was on poor Nancy and Tim as the deaths were seemingly identical, but it seemed like Tank's demise wasn't common knowledge so thankfully we weren't pestered by any morbid thrill-seekers coming to ask us about it.

Several determined souls had ventured into the lake to paddle board or swim, shrieking as they braved the cool, dark water.

"Fancy a dip?" I asked, grinning at Min.

"Are you mad? It'll be freezing. Look at those people getting out. They're blue, and shivering."

"What, you scared?" I teased.

"I'm not scared. I'm just not stupid. We'll never warm up again."

"I could put more wood on the fire so we'd be toasty soon enough."

"Then you're on!"

"What!? I was only joking."

"Ha! Now who's laughing? Come on, it was your idea, so let's do it."

"You aren't messing around?"

"It'll be like you said. Something different. And going for a cool dip always makes you super energised afterwards. I dare you."

"Then let's do it."

Giggling, we hurried over to Vee, disturbing Anxious who went from comatose to excited in a heartbeat, and began jumping around inside Vee while we struggled out of our clothes and into our swimming costumes. In her excitement, Min forgot about her usual insistence on not seeing each other naked, and I almost had a coronary when I turned to find her slipping on her bikini top. She caught me looking and smiled, and for one minute I let my hopes get high before she hastily fastened up and and turned her back to me, but not before I caught her smiling and accepted the cheeky wink she sent my way with a nervous swallow.

"Min, you are beautiful."

"Just watch yourself, mister. You pervert."

"Hey, I'm no pervert. You're the one prancing around in the nude in here. It's too small for us to both get changed at the same time, especially with the bed down. There's like only enough space for a small dog, not two adults."

"Then stop rolling around on the bed and get out of here." Min stepped outside and wrapped a towel around her waist, so I finished getting ready, slid off the bed onto the tiny square of floor space, and battled outside with Anxious doing his utmost to trip me up. I reached back inside and grabbed my own towel then built up the fire before we dashed across the path, down the grassy bank, and stopped at the shallow water's edge, both shivering.

"You first," ordered Min.

"Why me?"

"Because it was your idea. Off you go. I'll be right behind you."

"No way! You'll bottle it and leave me in there alone. Take my hand, and we'll go in together."

Bored by having to wait, Anxious launched into the water and landed with a splash then swam around merrily, tongue lolling, his little legs working hard. He lifted his head higher and barked encouragement, so not waiting as I knew we'd change our minds, we nodded to each other then ran into the water, shivering, but kept on going until it was up to our thighs, then released hands and dove under.

I gasped as I came up for air, the cold taking my breath away, but not as much as the sight of Min as she surfaced then stood, her skin glistening with the icy water as it ran down her body in rivulets. She smiled as she teased her hair back, and I wiped my eyes, afraid I was witnessing a mirage, rather than this possibly being real.

Right there in the water on a balmy evening, standing in my swimming shorts, I felt truly happy in a way I never had before. Life was perfect, this moment was perfect, and I felt close to bursting into tears the feeling became so overwhelming. Min must have felt something similar as we both waded close then held hands and stared into each other's eyes as Anxious trod water between us, head between our outstretched arms.

"A family," was all I managed to say.

"A family," Min agreed, her face glowing with happiness.

The tension released, we laughed as we splashed about then braved it and swam with Anxious across the lake, reaching the other side in under a minute and gratefully wading to the shore by the death slide, breathing fast, chests heaving.

Min beamed, and declared, "That was so much fun!" before wringing out her hair and shaking like Anxious.

"Awesome! And not as freezing as I expected it to be." I squeezed my beard, then my hair, the cold of it hanging down my back making me shiver.

"Let's swim back, then go and dry off. It's too cold to stand around."

"I don't care. I could happily stay here all night."

"Not me. I'm getting goosebumps." Min shivered, I ogled, then she laughed at me before splashing back into the depths and diving under, Anxious on her heels.

I followed after them and we raced back, Min beating me, Anxious second, and I waded to the shore and caught up with them then we dried off quickly, wrapped the towels around our waists, and hurried to the warmth of the fire. We rubbed our hands together and stood as close to the fire as we could, warming instantly as the flames licked high into the darkening sky.

Neither of us spoke; we both knew how the other felt. Energised, buoyant, our bodies thrumming with adrenaline and the high of feeling alive, the extremes of temperature eliciting an unconscious response within, the endorphins racing around our systems. We grinned at each other through the flames, our skin glowing and tingling as the fire warmed us to our very core.

Min glanced to the side and frowned.

"What's wrong?"

"I thought I saw someone," she shrugged. "Maybe Kelly."

"Probably going for a walk."

"She was crouched over, like she didn't want to be seen. On the other side of the lake by the death slide. She ducked under the frame for it. I wonder what she's doing?"

"Maybe we should go and take a look? It might be important."

"Should we? It's been a perfect evening so far, and forgetting about the awful things that happened was just what we needed. Do you think she might be responsible for the deaths?"

"I honestly don't know. I like Kelly, and she seems on the level, but maybe we should check that she isn't doing anything dodgy." I found myself retrieving Anxious' lead without even thinking about it, then returned to them and clipped him on so he wouldn't give us away.

With a nod, we hurried into the shadows then made our way around the lake, keeping away from the path and using trees or vehicles for cover. As we approached the death slide, we saw Kelly dash towards the woods where we'd found the bag. With a quick discussion, we decided to follow, both of us shivering, and we must have made a strange sight if anyone spotted us creeping along in our swimming costumes, looking like we were taking the dog for a walk but trying to be like ninjas, hardly the ideal outfits as Min's red bikini wasn't exactly discreet. I stayed behind her to keep an eye on things, my thoughts drifting from what Kelly was up to as my eyes focused on the much more alluring sight in front of me.

Min turned suddenly, scowling. "Are you staring at my bum?" she demanded, hands on hips.

"Bum? What bum? Do you have one? I hadn't even noticed. And if I was, it was only so I could follow you and keep you safe."

"Safe from what? Killer bum pinchers?"

"Um, maybe," I offered, unable to think straight.

"Stay beside me. You're putting me off."

"Putting you off what?"

"Being a ninja. I'm trying to stay out of sight."

"With a bum like that? Good luck."

"Are you saying my bum's big?"

"No, of course not. It's perfect."

"So you were staring?"

I was not going to win this, so admitted, "Yes, I was staring at your bottom. Happy now?"

"Yes." With a sweet smile, Min pulled me to her side.

We crouched, then followed after the distant figure of Kelly who was acting just as ridiculous as us and trying not be seen as she approached where the bag was found.

As we got closer, it became obvious that Kelly was trying to reach the trees and possibly the bag, but there would be absolutely no chance of her getting there unseen. Kim and Jim were there, along with Frank and Mark, plus Mike Almond and a whole host of official looking men and women, some in uniform, others plain clothes. There were also teams setting up a white tent and more people approaching across the field. Kelly paused, then turned around and headed back the way she'd come, right towards us.

"She's spotted us," I noted.

"Should we run away?" Min's eyes darted this way and that like a wild animal caught in the headlights, and I had to stifle a snigger. Clearly, I didn't do a very good job as she asked, "What's so funny?"

"Why would we run away? She knows we're here, so there's no point. At least this should get taken seriously now, as Kim and Jim obviously reached the right people and they're investigating. I wonder what will happen now?"

"More trouble, I bet. Are you sure we shouldn't hide?"

"Min, she's right there."

"Um, hey, guys. What are you doing here?" Kelly took in our peculiar choice of outfit and frowned, clearly confused.

"What about you?" asked Min. "Why are you here? We were just out for a walk to exercise Anxious."

"In your swimming costumes? Nice bikini, by the way." Kelly looked Min up and down, causing Min to become self-conscious, and she squeezed behind me.

"Yes, we were hot. We had a swim, then stood by the fire, but thought we'd have a stroll. So, what are you up to?"

"I bumped into the two young cops earlier and they told me about the bag that was found. It sounded interesting, so I figured I'd come and see what the fuss was all about. There are too many people there, though, so I changed my mind."

"They told you?" I was surprised, but even as I spoke I understood that they were young, excited, and believed Kelly to be innocent, although clearly involved as it was her business partner who was dead.

"Yes. I was rather surprised, but they were buzzing and Jim let it slip, then they filled me in. You found the bag and there was a load of weird stuff in it. What was it?"

Min and I looked to one another for guidance, but neither of us said anything so eventually Min told Kelly all about it. It felt right, and I relaxed more for trusting her, but what Kelly said next changed everything.

"That cop, Frank, is into antiques. Mike too. They dabble, is what they call it. I only know because when they used to have a stall they were always boasting about how little they paid for things at car boot sales and how much they sold them for. They were mostly into jewellery."

"So it might be theirs? And now they're the ones doing the investigating? This isn't right at all," said Min, gnawing her lip.

"It doesn't mean they killed three people," I reminded them. "Lots of people buy and sell things. And let's not forget there was a gun. I doubt they'd be foolish enough to risk getting caught with that. They'd lose their jobs and get sent down for years."

"But it does make them suspects. Mike, his brother, and Mark. They could all be involved."

"Not Mark. He's a good guy," said Kelly. "And he wasn't involved in the pie business. Just Mike and Frank. And they were really into antiques, like I said. A buckle, rings, and even the Zippo might be worth a lot, and they're exactly the kind of things you find at car boot sales."

"Maybe, but you're both forgetting one thing."

"What?" they asked.

"The bag was hidden. Why would they bury it here? What would be the point if it was just random things they picked up cheaply?"

"Maybe they worried it would get mislaid, or they'd be in trouble for having it. Maybe it's stolen goods."

"Again, why hide it here? There'd be less chance of it being discovered if it was in their own vehicles. Now look what's happened. Swarms of officials, their bosses, teams for forensics, and a massive tent erected. No, I can't see it. They may seem like idiots, but they aren't dumb."

"No, just lazy," hissed Kelly. "Or maybe it wasn't incompetence that made them put the deaths down as natural causes. Maybe it was because they did it out of revenge or something." Kelly shrugged. She was guessing, and we knew it.

"Let's get out of here. The last thing we need is to get cornered by them. I imagine they're in a very bad mood and looking to take it out on someone." I led the way with Anxious now unclipped so he could run around, so we headed back to the lake then said goodbye to Kelly and returned to the warmth of the fire.

Unfortunately for me, but much warmer for Min, she changed back into her clothes then I did likewise. We arranged our chairs around the fire and settled down, assuring each other there would be no more snooping for the evening.

Cold wine and a warm fire along with perfect company made for a fantastic evening, and we had a great time chatting and chilling, again having decided there would be no talk of murder or endlessly discussing the potential culprit. There were no end of suspects, and I was certain that the following day would bring a few more to add to the list. Hopefully, we could all learn what the coroner's reports had to say about the deaths, as long as someone was willing to share the information with us.

Min was in good spirits, but there was still that underlying sadness because of her indecision about the future. I understood where she was coming from and would remain true to my word and not try to sway her if she chose not to live with us, but I hoped that wouldn't be the case. It was hard, but I had to see it from her point of view.

I'd already utterly transformed my life and become a nomad, but she'd taken the last few years since we split to find her place in the world, settle into a new way of living without us being a couple, and got her life on track. Now the thought of upending everything and basically starting all over again was understandably terrifying. I knew she loved me, wanted us to be together, and was sure I'd changed and would never revert back to my old ways, but it was still a very big ask.

But deep down, I think we both knew her mind was already made up. She was just scared of doing it. I smiled at the thought, and wondered what the future would be like when we were back together again. Would Vee cope with Min's proclivity for leaving things everywhere and the inevitable damage as stuff flew around the van? What would Anxious do without as much room on the bed?

I was looking forward to finding out, and starting what would be the true adventure of our lives.

When bedtime came around, we packed away a few odds and ends then joined Anxious on the bed. He huffed and complained as he had to squeeze between us, but we cuddled up, I turned out the light, and as a family we drifted off, dreaming of the future and what it might bring.

The morning was bright and very warm by seven, so I rose without disturbing Min, and took Anxious outside so he could have a pee and I made the morning emergency dash to the toilets. I vowed to get a portable toilet, space be damned. I could store it in the gazebo and disguise it as a seat like I'd seen a few people do on YouTube. But then I'd have the hassle of lugging containers of wee around the place to empty it, so by the time I'd trudged back I had no clue what my plans were, only knowing that I had to come up with something by the summer or Min would be changing her mind and remaining in the ease and comfort of her house.

Chapter 14

I made coffee in the gazebo, assuming the smells wafting into Vee would wake Min, but there was no sign of her as I poured out the dark, smoky liquid and sipped. Stepping out into the sunshine, I watched as the world around me slowly woke and life continued for another day. At least for some. For others, there would be no more chances to appreciate the majesty of the world and all it had to offer for anyone willing to take a step back, silence their inner demons for a while, and simply stand and stare, listen, and take it all in.

People even more crazy than me and Min were already in the water; I couldn't imagine how cold it would be now. I smiled at their hushed shrieks, the swimmers braving the dark depths to invigorate their minds and bodies. Pink skin and happy faces were the result as they hurried from the shallows and wrapped up in towels or the dry robes that had suddenly become all the rage with the vanlife community. What was great to see were the number of others wearing plastic clogs of all description, not just Crocs, so at least I wasn't alone in my choice of footwear.

After my coffee, I decided to have another one on the go so poured it into my new sipping flask and called for Anxious then headed off for a wander around the site. Always keen, the little guy bounced from the van, yawning as his ears flapped and his tail wagged manically. I pocketed his lead just in case, checked for the poo bags which were in various pockets, then we headed off along the path.

The stalls were silent, the curtains down on the gazebos, but I heard clattering and quiet conversations from behind a few of them as the vendors prepared their wares for the day ahead. It promised to be a real scorcher, so they would be excited about it being a busy day with hundreds of new arrivals keen to part with their money in exchange for a cheese pie and a chance to relax somewhere nice.

After the row of stalls, I wandered along the first line of campervans, smiling and nodding at the people sitting outside with coffees or pottering around organising things. It was always a strange experience seeing others who lived as I did, the nods always knowing, the smiles always saying more than they did with others. It was as though we shared a secret, which I supposed we did, and there was always this underlying sense of camaraderie. Of us exchanging a simple look that held so much meaning, like we'd cracked the code to life and couldn't help showing off.

It's like when you go to the beach and the car parks closest to the paths or the water always have a few campervans right at the front. The owners get there early so they can sit outside their vans with a cuppa and smile at people passing by, feeling smug and showing off the fact they can make a drink anywhere, any time, and even take a nap if they want.

There must have been a good few hundred campervans here now, and most likely more would arrive for the final day of this little festival that was big on pies, death slides, and, unfortunately, murder. Many early risers were already doing the rounds of the vans, peering through windows if the curtains or doors were open, even chatting with the owners and taking a look inside, swapping tips on vanlife—there were so many it could make the head of the uninitiated spin with how much there was to think about.

But beyond all that, which was mostly background noise and concerns to what really mattered, there was this undeniable, unmistakable look in their eyes that I knew I shared. A deep-seated, almost impossible to describe inner happiness that radiated.

We'd figured out something others might spend their whole lives searching for and never even understand they craved.

Freedom!

We were free in a way we had never been before we began this very different way of life. Yes, it was a struggle. Hard, physical, cramped, sometimes annoying, wet, or unbearably hot, uncomfortable, problematic. Stressful when your home broke down and you realised you had nowhere to live while the garage took a week to fix your vehicle and the bill made you want to tear your hair out. But above all else was a real sense of liberation that crept up on you day by day until you finally found yourself in the gang, smiling smugly at other vanlifers, sharing the secret with a knowing nod or a quick, "Nice van, mate," as you passed by, a spring in your step.

The young officers, Kim and Jim, weren't at their marquee, so I hoped they were alright and hadn't been pulled off the job. We changed direction and headed out into the grounds and across the field towards the site of so much excitement yesterday. The large white tent that had been erected around our find was gone, and I couldn't see any crime scene tape, but there were quite a few people still there so I decided to go over and see what was happening. Best to get this over and done with, and deal with whatever Mike had to say without involving Min as there was no point us both getting stressed by the man.

Anxious sniffed the air then ran off ahead, tail spinning, so there was obviously someone there he liked, which boded well. I slowed, leaving him to enjoy some adoration, while I checked around to see if anything else might have happened. The voices were too far away to make out, but a squeal of delight made me certain that at least Kim was there and giving Anxious a nice fuss.

By the time I arrived, Anxious was upside down, tongue lolling, legs akimbo, sighing as Kim and Jim rubbed his belly.

"Hey." I smiled at the eager cops, then glanced at the three more jaded men standing around staring at us with a look of distaste.

"Hi, Max," said Kim as she stood.

"Nice day," said Jim brightly, then glanced over his shoulder before frowning at me. He leaned in close as he stood, and said, "They weren't happy, but we did the right thing."

"That's great. Busy night?"

They explained that they'd been allowed to stay while the teams went over the satchel and its contents, then everything was checked for fingerprints before being bagged up for more in-depth study at the station, then the entire area was searched but nothing else was found. Their boss had insisted they stay at the scene, and were told to do what they could today and speak to as many people as possible.

"That sounds great. Well done." Both beamed, clearly pleased with how things had gone so far. "What news about the postmortems? Have they been done?"

"We just got the results. The coroner's assistant called and said they'd been up half the night after they were told to fast-track them as there's definitely something weird going on here." Kim moved closer and whispered, "Not that Mike was happy about that. He got a right earful in front of everyone and nearly quit there and then. He came around a little though."

"So, what were the results?"

Kim and Jim looked to each other for support; something was clearly amiss.

"We aren't meant to say. We got told not to engage with you. To do our jobs and leave the detective work to Mike and the guys," said Jim glumly. "You'll have to ask them, I'm afraid."

We turned to the three men who had remained still and watching us the whole time. I nodded to the young ones, then we wandered over to them and I said hello. I got a few grunts and a polite hi from Mark, the only decent one out of the three, then waited. The telling off I'd expected didn't come, and instead Mark explained that they'd need a statement but I could give it to Jim and Kim in a moment.

"Then you can bugger off and stop interfering," hissed Mike.

"Cool it, Mike," warned Mark.

"I wasn't interfering. We went for a walk and Anxious discovered the satchel."

"And you handled a loaded, deadly weapon. You should know better," said Frank.

"You're right, and I'm sorry. Any fingerprints or leads? What do you think it means?"

"We have no prints and no leads. Whoever left it here clearly planned on retrieving it at some point, but as to what it means, we're at a loss."

"Possibly someone into antiques?" I asked, watching closely for their reactions.

"Doubtful, as most of it was junk. The buckle was only silver-plated," said Mike, surprising me by offering some detail. "The rings were your standard gold and silver, but nothing special, and the coin was worth exactly ten pence."

"My brother's right," said Frank. "Not that it's any of your business. You were warned to stay away and yet here we find ourselves, with you once again in the middle of things. Keep clear of this, Max, and let my brother investigate."

"Ah, so you are going to investigate now?"

"Don't have any choice now, do I? This was done and dusted until you stuck your nose in again. Now, because of the satchel, my boss is all over me like a nasty rash. He won't be satisfied until we've questioned everyone here and come up with an answer he finds satisfactory. Thanks a bunch, Max." Mike wandered off, sipping his coffee from a paper cup, somehow managing to make it an angry gesture, the coffee dribbling down his chin into his overnight stubble. To be fair, all of them looked exhausted and were still in the same clothes as yesterday, so I assumed they'd been up all night dealing with various matters so weren't best pleased with me for that either.

"What's the plan then?" I asked, remaining calm, not letting Mike's sour mood affect mine.

"Ask around, see if we can uncover a motive, then get the hell out of here and go home for a shower and some decent grub." Frank glared at me like it was my fault, then left in a huff to join his brother.

"Ignore them. They're grumpy because they have to do some work," said Mark.

"And like to take it out on us," grumbled Jim.

"Yeah, I know, and I'm sorry. Look, this will be over by tomorrow at the latest as the festival closes, so bear with them for another day. I'll do my best to keep them out of your way." Mark smiled at them and added, "You've been doing a great job and handled yourselves well last night, especially with the top brass breathing down our necks." Mark pulled me to one side and we walked off to talk in private.

"Problem?" I asked.

"Where do I start?" he sighed, rubbing at his head. "I can't wait to see the back of that pair. I've worked with Frank for so many years and I've had enough of his lax, mean attitude. Bring on retirement is what I say. Nearly there."

"So it hasn't been the best working relationship?"

"No, it hasn't. What with him and Mike always up to one hair-brained scheme or another and trying to earn a few extra quid, it's been a tough slog. But this is me nearly done. A final stint this weekend, then it's retirement and plenty of holidays in the sun. Can't wait."

"And Frank's retiring too?"

"He is. Hopefully, I'll never have to see his sorry face again. He has a few more months, though, but I'll be gone. Happy days."

"Mark, I know this is an impossible question for you to answer, but could they be involved in this? Are they clean cops? I heard they used to run a pie business, and that they're into antiques. That's suspicious, right?"

Mark's colour rose and his fists bunched, but the flash of anger was short-lived and he exhaled sharply then forced himself to relax. "Okay, I get where you're coming from and why you asked. They're incompetent and insufferable, don't want to work hard, and are always looking for an easy way out. But that's as far as it goes. They're not dirty cops, Max. I turn a blind eye to a lot of what they do, or don't do, but they don't take bribes, don't break the law, and what I hate the most about your question is that it implies I would let them get away with it."

"I'm sorry, and I know it was a terrible thing to ask, but I wanted to be sure."

"Then now you know."

"Can you tell me the autopsy results? Are you allowed?"

"Not really, but the sooner this thing is cleared up the better. Don't tell the others, but I'm on your side here, Max. If you can figure it out then go for it. Stay out of our way, don't let them know you're involved, but do what you can."

"I will. You can count on it. So, the results?"

"Inconclusive."

"For all three?"

"I'm afraid so. I spoke to the coroner myself a few hours ago. She wasn't happy with her and the team having to work all night, but it is what it is. The man under your van, Tank, died from his wounds. They were in keeping with what you'd expect by being stuck under a vehicle. His chest was compressed, and he suffocated because he couldn't breathe and punctured a lung too. Most likely, it was when you went over the speed bumps. There's not much room under those vans. The broken neck was what finally did for him."

"That's an awful way to go."

"It sure ain't pretty."

"And the other two?"

"As I said, inconclusive. No sign of foul play, but it can't be ruled out. Seems like it was a heart attack for both of them. No drugs, or alcohol, or any strange substances, but the tests are always limited. Unless you know what you're looking for, you can only check for so much before it gets too costly. Nancy seemingly had a heart attack, two actually, and Tim passed from a single one. At least it was quick."

"But the deaths are suspicious?"

"Of course they are! Three people dead, two of them brothers, the third direct competition to the other company. It's suspicious alright. But I'm not the detective and don't get to call the shots. That was up to Mike until your discovery brought the head honchos down on us all. Now they want every stone looked under and for Mike to be a hundred percent sure it was a series of very unfortunate accidents."

"And do you think they were? Come on, Mark, there's no way three people die and it's a coincidence."

"I know, but like I said, it isn't down to me. I'll do what I can, try to light a fire up their... Well, you know what I mean. Tank was bad news by all accounts, and always up to something. To me, that seems like an accident, but who knows? As for the other two, yes, it's suspicious, but it could genuinely have been a coincidence. The heat, the stress, the panic over making those stupid big pies might have been the final straw if they were both susceptible to heart trouble."

"But did they have any ongoing medical problems? Any history of heart issues?"

"Not that we're aware of, no."

"So what happens now?"

"I'll tell you what happens now. You do your thing, stay away from us so there's no bother, and I'll try my best to ensure we get to the truth. This bag has me worried. It's one thing to have three stiffs on our hands, quite another to know someone's hiding guns. It makes no sense."

"I'm sure you'll figure it out," I laughed, slapping his back.

"Don't count on it. I'll be spending my time trying to keep those two fat lumps from swigging coffee, eating pies, and just waiting out the day in the shade until they can give up and go home and never think about any of this again. That's their plan. I'll do what I can, but if there's any chance of this getting solved I'm afraid it's most likely down to you and that lovely wife of yours."

"Ex-wife," I corrected.

"Yeah, sure, Max. You and your ex are our only hope, and it pains me so much to say that. What's this job come to, eh? I'm relying on a stranger, and an amateur, to solve something my people should be fighting over to figure out."

"At least Kim and Jim are good people. They've really stepped up. I wouldn't be surprised if they uncover the killer before any of us."

"Let's hope so. They're great kids and deserve a break. At least us old duffers will be out of the picture soon and this new generation will hopefully step up and do a better job than us old-timers. Max, it breaks my heart to see cops give up like my partner and his brother. It shouldn't be like this, but the job grinds you down and some can't handle it."

"Then they shouldn't be police."

"True. It's an imperfect world, though, and we don't always get what we want. Take it easy, Max, and good luck." With a weary sigh, Mark returned to the others.

I retrieved Anxious, who had remained upside down and wagging the whole time, clearly expecting never-ending adoration, then said goodbye to the two young hopefuls and strolled back towards the site. I had a lot to think about; Anxious not so much.

Chapter 15

Min was awake when we got back, brimming with energy after a great sleep. The kettle was on, and everything was in order, so I kissed her good morning then sat and explained what had happened while we had our drinks. Like me, she was shocked but not really surprised by the outcome with the police, but she was taken aback by Mark's acceptance and even encouragement regards our involvement.

We went over the causes of death, agreeing it was likely Tank died how the coroner had reported, but when it came to the other two, it simply didn't ring true.

"Nobody believes it was natural causes," I said.

"Of course they don't. It's so dumb. And now the case is in the hands of that cretin yet again. How can his boss let him be so flaky?"

"Because he's been around so long and they know they can't fire him. I assume they give him cases they're already convinced won't lead to anything, so he can skive off without them getting stressed about his bad attitude. He'll be retired soon along with the others, but it's very disappointing to know there are people like that who are meant to protect us."

"Max, don't be too pessimistic. I know you've had run-ins and issues with other detectives, but when you think about it, he's the only one who's actually been bad at his job. The others meant well, and worked hard, even if they didn't want you around. This guy is a one-off."

"You're right. The police have been great overall and do a fine job. I'm just being grumpy. Mike Almond doesn't put people in a good mood. I vowed I wouldn't let him or Frank get to me, so let's forget about them and decide what we're going to do today."

"What I want to do, and don't laugh,"

I made the Scout's salute, and promised, "I won't."

"I'd like to learn how to make a pie."

"A pie?"

"Yes, a pie." Min's steely gaze bored into me, daring me to make fun.

I felt itty bitty pieces of my brain begin to melt under the strain of returning the look, her power on a par with Mum's, which was no mean feat. "Um, why?"

"Because you're so good at cooking and I never get to make you anything nice."

"You're a fine cook."

"Max, I am not. Ever since I've had to make my own meals, I've come to realise that I am not a good cook at all. I'm adequate. I never think of anything exciting to make, and what I do prepare is nice enough, but it never tastes like your food. I want to at least master something, and I figured that since we're here with these pie-making experts, I'd finally learn how to make something a professional would be proud of."

"Makes sense."

"I'm going to find Kelly and ask her to teach me. She said yesterday that she'd be making fresh pies early this morning in their kitchen but that she'd also be making a few batches here. They have a portable kitchen in their trailer just in case they need to make them at festivals, and it attracts customers as the smell is out of this world according to her."

"You didn't want me to show you how to make the best pie ever?" I teased.

"No way! You know how you get. All controlling and getting angry if I don't do it exactly how you say I should. You forget that everyone has their own way of doing things and turn super bossy."

"But when you ask to be shown how to make something, you're meant to follow the directions given. You can't improvise if you haven't nailed the process."

"See, you've started already. We've had more arguments when cooking together than at any other point."

"Only because you don't follow what I say. That's not how it works."

"Of course it is," she said brightly, then blew me a kiss to show there were no hard feelings.

"So, you'd rather have a stranger show you how to make something as simple as a pie instead of me? That hurts, Min. It cuts deep. You besmirch my honour and my pride as a chef."

"Liar! You're relieved I don't want your help. It's written all over your face."

I laughed and admitted, "I am. You're the worst student ever. You keep changing the ingredients and won't even do things in the right order."

"I like to improvise."

"You can't always improvise, especially not until you've mastered how it's meant to be done."

"So I'm going to get Kelly to teach me, and then you can sample the greatest pie in the world. All I need is an oven, and, er, um, what else do I need?"

"A massive spoonful of luck?" I suggested, ducking as the laser beams strobed across the top of my head, singing my hair.

"Hey, that's not fair. Anyway, I'm going to learn and you'll taste it and be super jealous."

"Maybe you could even write up the recipe for me?"

"Are you being cheeky?"

"No, absolutely not. Kelly's pies, and the others we tasted, were awesome. You're right, they're professionals and they focus on one thing until they make it perfect. I wouldn't mind knowing their secrets either."

"Then prepare to be astounded."

"Min, there's one flaw in your plan."

"What's that?" Min looked crestfallen.

I hurried to answer. "You haven't even asked Kelly, have you? What if she doesn't have the time, or is too stressed to teach you?"

"She said yesterday that she'd show me. Offered, actually. Said it would be nice to have a distraction, and she was happy to have made a new friend."

"Then that's great. You go for it."

"I will!" Min didn't move.

"Go on then."

"I'm going." She stayed put.

I raised an eyebrow. "Today?"

"Right now." She sipped her coffee.

"See you later," I chuckled.

"Bye." Still no movement.

Anxious cocked his head, confused. So did I.

"Have fun," I sniggered.

"Um, will you come with me?"

"Whatever for?"

"Because I feel silly going on my own. If we both go, we can pretend it's about the murders."

"Let me get this straight. You'll feel silly going to a pre-arranged offer to show you how to make a pie, but won't be embarrassed to rock up and start grilling her about the murders if you have backup?"

"Now you say it like that, it sounds daft, but you know what I mean."

"You didn't ask her, did you?" I accused, pointing my finger and smiling.

"I did too! She said it would be fun."

"Then what's the issue?"

"We need to see what she says about everything. And, well, I'm still not a hundred percent about her. She's shifty. I want you there in case anything happens. I don't want to face-plant into what will obviously be the most magnificent pie ever made."

"Obviously," I agreed, smirking at Anxious who coughed politely to mask his guffaw.

"Oi, you two, stop making fun of me." Min pouted and lowered her gaze.

"Sorry, we were only messing around. Of course we'll come. We won't stay while you make your pie, but it would be good to catch up and see if Kelly has any news. Shall we have breakfast first?"

"I'm not very hungry. Maybe just cereal or toast. I could do eggs."

"I think I'll stick with toast. We'll probably eat loads later, so best keep room. Especially for your pie."

"Great idea." Min nodded, a faraway look in her eyes.

Anxious and I exchanged a concerned glance while her thoughts were elsewhere. We both hoped the pie was a success. Min hated that she'd never been the best cook, and took it very personally when she had a fail, even though she knew it wasn't a reflection on her as a person. Just like it was no big deal if you messed up the plumbing for a simple repair, you still felt inadequate somehow, even though everyone can't be an expert at everything.

After breakfast and a freshen up, we pottered around and sorted a few things out. I cleaned out the fire now it was cold while Min re-arranged a few things inside Vee to free up some much-needed space, which got my hopes up as it was like she was practising for when she moved in. If she moved in, I had to tell myself.

Ready to face the day proper, and dressed in cut-offs and vests, our tans deep, skin glowing, we looked the epitome of health and vitality. I felt fresh and alive, full of energy, the glorious day lifting my mood until I was fit to burst.

"What's got into you?" asked Min as I stared into the clear blue sky and laughed at nothing in particular.

"I'm happy. It's a lovely day, the sun's out, people are laughing and joking, there are pets, campervans, everyone's keen to party, and I have the best company in the world with me. What's to feel glum about?"

"You're right. It is a wonderful day, and you do have the best company." Min smiled and kissed my cheek, then patted my bum.

I turned to her in shock and she reddened. "You haven't done that for a long time," I grinned.

"No, sorry. It was automatic. Like I used to do. Like you used to do too. A sign of affection. I shouldn't have. It wasn't right."

"Min, don't be daft. It was nice. Comforting. Feel free." To ease her embarrassment, I stuck my bottom out and bent over a little, so she gave it a good wallop and giggled.

"You silly man. Come on, let's go."

With a spring in our step, and joy in our hearts, we held hands as we ambled along the path.

The stalls were beginning to open now it was ten, although foot traffic was still light at the early hour. It would be lunchtime before the crowds built, and the afternoon when things really took off once the pie rolling competition got underway. Apparently, it always drew massive crowds, with children and adults alike crowding into the water to try and catch the pies as they sailed off the end of the death slide. Judges would be dotted around in the lake, too, to measure the distance, but the real draw was to see the pies go flying and to try to nab a freebie before it got soggy. It sounded fun, in a typically quirky small town way, and I was looking forward to it.

Kelly's was yet to open, the sign up and the marquee front drawn back, but the tables were bare and there was nobody around. We called out, but there was no answer. Concerned, as why wouldn't we be after yesterday, we slipped down the side to the work van they used to cook in and to serve pies at some festivals.

We almost walked straight into Kelly where she was sitting in a camping chair, leaning forward, knees nearly touching Tina, their hands held tight together.

"Sorry, we're interrupting. Didn't mean to intrude." I was already backing away, Min likewise, but Anxious had other ideas.

Never one to pick up on subtleties, or the downright obvious suggestion to "Leave it!" when sausages were involved, he raced between the women and jumped into Kelly's lap then sat and stared at her, waiting for her to turn to putty in his paws and offer up the love she undoubtedly had for him.

"It's fine, Max," said Kelly, smiling at the little guy, then us, before glancing at Tina and receiving a very tired nod. "I was filling Tina in on what happened here. She's been up all night waiting to hear the results of Tim's, er, you know."

"The autopsy," sighed Tina.

"We just heard," I said. "We're so sorry."

"We really are. You must be exhausted, you poor thing." Min stepped forward as I shifted position to the side, and Kelly and Tina shunted their chairs back so there was space for everyone

"I feel so drained, but like I'm not really here. It's a very weird experience. Too tired, I suppose. Kelly was telling me how much help you've both been, and about what happened yesterday. I can't believe Nancy died in exactly the same way. No way can that be coincidence. And now this satchel. With a gun, no less! Terrible." Tina fiddled with her shirt, a simple cotton affair over which she wore an apron like Kelly's. Was she planning on working today?

"Have you come to work?" I couldn't help asking. "Don't you need to get some sleep?"

"I didn't want to leave poor Kelly to do everything. Today's a big day and will be very busy. I'm so pleased we won the competition yesterday, but we still have today to get through."

"I told you, I'll be fine. I can handle it."

"What else would I do? Tim's still in the morgue. The police are investigating, apparently, although after what Kelly told me about the detective, it doesn't sound like they're going to do much."

"I spoke to everyone involved earlier, and things aren't as bleak as they seem. Mike might not like it, but his boss is breathing down his neck and he's going to do what he can. But it's not just him. The others involved, especially the younger cops, are keen to figure this out. Hang in there, and let's see what the day brings."

"That's reassuring," sighed Tina, not looking like she believed it, which was understandable.

She'd missed out on most of what went on yesterday, but was around for enough, and heard enough via Kelly, to have her doubts about her husband's death ever getting solved.

"We hate to ask," said Min, "but is there anything you can tell us that might help? Anyone who had it in for Tim? Nancy too? Any arguments lately with anyone? Something out-of-the-ordinary? Anything at all?"

"Nothing unusual. There's always a few arguments with others at events like this, but only the usual nonsense. We all mostly get on, even share tips sometimes, but I'm afraid to say people like Nancy and Jake aren't very likeable and they hated that we won last year."

"So there's nothing you can think of that might result in this?" I asked. "What about Tank? Anything unusual been going on there?"

"Nothing at all. As far as I know, they hadn't spoken for ages. Tank was bad news, which I know Kelly told you. He was nothing but trouble for our family and our business. He was terrible with money, and often homeless. I don't even know where he was living. Maybe I should ask the police if they found out."

"Maybe. Could it be tied up with him?"

Tina frowned as she considered the question. "I don't see how. Even if he was in debt to some dodgy people, it would have nothing to do with us. He hasn't worked here for a long time."

"But would he have lied? Maybe told someone he could get money off his brother?"

"It's possible."

Kelly coughed to get our attention, then asked, "How would that explain why Tim and Nancy were killed? And how was it done anyway? And this bag is a real problem. What's that all about?"

"We aren't sure what any of it means," I admitted. "Knowing as much as we can is the best way to try to figure this out. The more information we have, the better. Sorry to intrude, and we should go, but we will try our best to help."

"That's so kind of you," said Tina. "Thank you so much."

"Min, you will hang around, though, won't you?" asked Kelly.

"Now doesn't seem like the right time," said Min. "And you have to set up the stall. Have you finished baking?"

Kelly stood, indicated her grubby apron, and said, "I've been up since all hours getting everything ready. There are a few things to do in the van, but mostly it's a matter of setting everything out. Why don't you help us with that, then we can do your masterclass in making the perfect pie."

"If you're sure. It feels wrong after what's happened."

"We insist," said Tina. "It will do us good, and I know I need the distraction. It will be quiet for a few hours until close to lunch when everyone arrives, and the afternoon will be chaotic. We can handle it, we're used to it, but this morning let's take it easy and teach you all our secrets." Tina managed a weak wink and smile, so Min agreed to stay and help set up, then get her lesson.

Anxious and I said goodbye, and left them to it, emerging from the shade of the vehicles and marquees into a bright, busy morning by the lake, the foot traffic increasing as we wandered along the path with no direction in mind.

Was Tina on the level? Did she want to get rid of her husband and the competition? Could she be behind this?

Chapter 16

It was beginning to feel like a true festival experience, which I was surprised by. Usually, there was either music or comedy, but this particular relatively small event had none of that yet still had an incredible buzz. Maybe it was the weather, as for many it would be the first true warm and sunny day out of the year, and for most their first camping trip, or maybe it was the lake. Everyone was enjoying it already, and the death slide was incredibly busy.

The food was certainly a draw, but so were the various campervans and motorhomes ranging from tiny conversions to behemoths that I couldn't even figure out how they managed to navigate the narrow lanes. Everyone was smiling, many were already drinking even though it was mid-morning, and there were an awful lot of pies being consumed.

Buoyed by the atmosphere, it felt like a boys' day out as it was just me and Anxious. I decided to do a circuit of the lake to get some much-needed steps in as I'd foregone a workout this morning, so at a leisurely pace we wandered around the well-trodden path, my eyes scanning for anything of interest, the murders always foremost in my mind. I noted Mike moping about the place, not doing much of anything, with his brother and Mark talking to various stallholders—it looked very half-hearted and like they were just killing time.

Eventually, we made it over to the death slide on the opposite side of the lake to our pitch, and I marvelled at the amount of people climbing the gargantuan monstrosity with a smile on their faces rather than abject terror.

"Makes you wonder, eh?" said Dave, the man in charge, who appeared as if from nowhere from the confusing tangle of beams and girders, props and struts that formed the skeleton of the ride.

"I went down it yesterday and almost bottled it," I reminded him. "Your assistant shoved me off."

"Sorry about that. I had a stern word with him. You won't catch me going down it."

"Have you worked here long?"

Dave scratched at his neck, the skin tight, his face lined and dark from sun exposure. His hair was lanky and straggly, a dirty blond streaked with grey was the best way to describe it, and he smelled a little off. Grubby, oil-stained jeans and work boots with the steel toecaps poking through the worn leather made me assume he'd been here for years, but sometimes people surprised you.

"I run the thing. Own it. Well, kind of. It's tied in with the charity that owns and maintains the entire site. Built it, too, although I had help with that."

"This is yours, but you won't go down it?"

He laughed, then said, "It's a business. I used to run the smaller one, but it had seen better days, and I didn't want to risk any accidents. It was more for the pie competition than anything, although we always got people paying to have a go too. When I got offered a grant to build something bigger and better, I leaped at the chance. It's open for nine months of the year now, and they do a load of different events here, so I do alright. Doesn't mean I have to go on it, though, does it?" He stepped closer and peered up at me as though I might have something smart to say in reply.

"I suppose not. Is it safe?"

"Course it is. You wouldn't believe the amount of paperwork involved in things like this. All the inspections, the weekly reports I have to make, the certificates for safety tests. Mind you, it's not what happens going down that you have to worry about, is it? It's landing, and the lake, but so far so good." Dave glanced at his smart watch then tapped at it, frowning.

"Problem?" I asked, nodding to the watch.

"Nah, just checking. I think I told you I go running most days, and I was seeing what my step count was. Definitely need to do a run later. It's an incredible bit of kit. Stores everything. Next, it'll be making my dinner," he laughed.

"People do seem to enjoy your new death slide. So you've worked here a long time?"

"Years and years," he nodded, his head wobbling like it might topple sideways and never recover. "Seen it all. Mind you, this is a record turnout this year for the pie festival. It's the weather. If it's sunny and dry, everyone wants to come. Should be a good earner for me."

"I assumed the trust would own it. The site's run by a trust, isn't it?"

"Sure is, but they can't afford to pay for everything so they sub some things out. You gotta know what you're doing with these massive rides. Used to run fairgrounds back in the day, which makes this seem like easy street. It's a decent living and an honest one, plus I get to be outside all day and enjoy this great site. Lovely, isn't it?"

"It sure is. I bet you get to hear all the gossip, don't you?" I noted his sideways glance, the way his fingers clenched and the slight step away. He frowned, then a slow smile spread and he laughed, a deep gravelly roar like it could turn into a cough at any moment. I caught a whiff of sour whisky and coffee, and knew what he'd had for breakfast. It hardly inspired confidence in him being able to keep a watchful eye on things, but I supposed that was what the staff were for.

He stepped up to me again. I noted the bloodshot eyes and the way he kept rubbing his two fingers together. His index finger was blistered and calloused. Could it be from repeatedly firing a gun? "Exactly who are you?" he sneered, spittle in the corner of his mouth stuck to his lower lip somehow fascinating and gross at the same time.

"Just a guy walking his dog."

"I've seen you around, and you seem very pally with the cops. You an investigator? A detective?" He prodded at his teeth with a long, dirty nail, then smirked. "Ah, I know you. You're that bloke, the vanlife detective. Yeah, I heard some of the customers talking about you. This about the deaths? You think you know something, eh?"

"I'm a concerned citizen, yes. I promised I'd see if I could uncover anything, and a man was found under my van."

"Oh, that was you? You found that idiot, Tank? I mean, come on, who's called Tank?"

"You knew him?"

"Course I did. Everyone did. He used to be around all the time a few years back. Right troublemaker. Always up to no good. He was always bugging me about one hare-brained scheme or another. Asking for money. He came up with some right doozies, that guy. Total scammer. Into the drugs, too, so I heard. Always half-soaked and real fidgety type. He used to hang around by the death slide, pestering the chicks. Er, I mean, ladies. Thought he was God's gift, and for some bizarre reason the women did seem to like him. He had a way about him, did Tank. Proper smooth talker when he wanted to be. There were even rumours about him and his sister-in-law, and that other one who's part of High Pies."

"You mean Kelly? I got the impression they weren't the best of friends. Didn't they fire him?"

"Sure they did. Guy never could hold a job down. But why did they fire him, eh? Because he was inept, or because one or both of them were carrying on with him?"

"Are you sure about that?"

"Nah, just yanking your chain, mate. Can you imagine? Kelly's like twenty years younger than him or something. Smart girl, that one. Doesn't stand for fools or anyone who slacks off. I like her. Pretty too. A real looker. But I did hear gossip about them all carrying on. Probably just that though. Everyone likes some drama, right?"

"They sure do. What do you think happened? I'm sure you know about the way everyone died. What's your take on it as someone who probably gets to hear more than anyone else? I've seen you around, and you clearly know everyone."

He scratched his head, and I realised I hadn't introduced myself properly. "Oh, sorry, I'm Max."

"Dave, although I think I told you that already. Not sure if you remember, what with you being so stressed and all." We shook, then he scratched at his head again while he thought. "If I was a betting man, which I'm not, I'd say that Tank did something dumb and it was an accident. He was always trying to get cash, so most likely tried to sneak in rather than paying and came a cropper. As for the other two, sounds like poison to me. Something that makes them keel over dead. And the motive's obvious. Money. It's always money, right?"

"Sometimes. Who would stand to gain the most?"

"Kelly, or Nancy's husband. That Jake bloke. He'd inherit the business so would keep all the cash. He and his missus were always arguing. Maybe he'd had enough."

"What about the police? You hear anything about them?"

"Wow, you ask a lot of questions. Okay, I'll bite, but only because I want this solved too. It ain't good for business. Mike Almond's a total weirdo. Always standing around, hardly talking, never doing any work. I've met him a few times over the years, and never took to the guy. That old copper, Mark, is nice enough, but his partner is like Mike. Another loser."

"Thanks, Dave, it's been really helpful. Sorry to keep you from your work for so long."

"No bother, Max. You catch the killer, you hear me?"

"I'll try my best."

Anxious remained right on my heels as we left and continued our walk. It wasn't like him to ignore a new face, but he'd acted as if Dave wasn't even there. No sniffing, no whining for a fuss, not even a growl to show he didn't like him. He was, for the first time I could recall, utterly indifferent. Worried about my best buddy, I halted then squatted and studied him with concern. He cocked his head, wagged, then licked his nose.

I laughed; he was fine. Nevertheless, I asked, "Did you like Dave? The man we just met." Anxious glanced at Dave jogging on the spot, then looked at me and whined.

"Didn't you like the way he smelled?"

Smart guy that he was, Anxious batted at his nose with a paw, then yipped.

"But you didn't say anything, or even bark at him. Was he a bad man?"

Anxious lay down but kept his focus on me.

"Sorry, I'm confusing you. I know you can't understand everything, but you do know a lot. Was Dave the killer?"

Anxious sat and wagged, like I'd suggested a walk.

"Fair enough," I chuckled. "Some you win, some you lose. Come on, let's continue our stroll."

The encounter with Dave played on my mind. He was certainly what you would call a functional alcoholic, the smell and the jittery hands, the twitching and the burst blood vessels on his nose and cheeks were a clear sign, plus the hip flask sticking out of his back pocket, but he clearly had a sound business head on his shoulders. Would he have murdered three, or maybe two people for some reason? What could that have been?

I needed to know more about the possible relationships between the major players, but that might be pushing things too far in their time of grief as clearly they weren't all responsible for the deaths.

Or were they?

Maybe they got together and planned it? Like in that movie when people met on a train and agreed to kill each other's victim. I shook my head and smiled to myself; I was getting way too carried away with this.

Deciding I needed a distraction, we circumnavigated the lake. I perused the stalls, then stopped, caught off guard by seeing Jake manning Pie in the Sky's stall. He was chatting with customers, sometimes looking serious when they were clearly discussing Nancy's demise, but jolly and bright when serving those who clearly knew nothing about it. He certainly didn't look like a man in despair after losing the love of his life. I couldn't imagine what I'd be like if I lost Min or Anxious, but I knew for a fact I wouldn't be serving pies and joking around.

The queue snaked back along past other stalls, much to the chagrin of the owners, but I suppose the large banner declaring they'd won second place had something to do with it. I was tempted to try to have a chat, but it would be so brief there was little point. We continued on our merry way, only pausing once we arrived at High Pies' spot. The area was absolutely rammed. Hundreds of people must have arrived while we were walking, and now there was no denying the power of the previous day's competition. With a huge banner even larger than Jake's and declaring they were the winners, it drew crowds like I couldn't quite believe. Why did baking a big pie make you so special? Maybe there was good local news coverage, or maybe it was word of mouth about the quality. Whatever it was, it had worked, and they were flat out.

I smiled as I spotted Min who was sweating and flustered as she served the hungry masses, clearly having been roped in to help. Tina and Kelly were on the move constantly, serving, reloading the table with more pies, lifting the card reader when the signal went dodgy, or handing over change. The amount people were spending was eye-watering. Maybe I'd been in the wrong business all those years as a chef. I should have specialised and opened up my own business. No way! I didn't want that life. I wanted to enjoy the slow passing of the days, not hurry through them being stressed and waiting for it to be over.

I don't think I'd truly appreciated that until this very moment. That I never looked forward to the evenings more than the days any more. It always used to be waiting for work to be over, although that was always early morning working in kitchens, but rather, I enjoyed it all from the moment I awoke. What a luxury that was. No need to check my watch constantly or wish for a moment to myself. I had all the time in the world and thanked my lucky stars for such an existence.

With Min seemingly busy for a while, I snuck off feeling ever so slightly guilty, but it soon passed as she wasn't beholden to them and could do as she chose. We spent a fun hour chatting with vanlifers and admiring vehicles and setups, even discovering a few new gadgets to save space and caught up on some gossip and tips about good spots in the area that were either cheap or free if you didn't mind a spot of stealth camping.

It was still a sore issue with many people, and over the last year I'd been living this way I'd begun to notice more and more signs at car parks or beauty spots where overnight parking was strictly prohibited. I could see both sides of it, and knew it was mostly down to a few people giving everyone else a bad name.

One of the best tips I'd ever had was from a seasoned vanlifer and wild camping obsessive who said that wherever she stayed, she always made a point of litter picking at least a bagful of rubbish before she left so that the place was always nicer than when she arrived. If everyone did that, the coastline, the beauty spots, and the average street would be much nicer and maybe stealth camping and overnight stays in vans wouldn't be seen as a nuisance. The few times I'd strayed from campsites I'd done exactly that, but never felt quite as relaxed or settled as at campsites as I was always worried I'd be asked to move along, and besides, you couldn't set up your gazebo and fire pit if you were in a lay-by!

Heading back to base through a field now rammed with tents and vans, I tripped on a guy rope and went flying face first. Panicked, I reached out for I don't know what, and somehow managed to grab hold of something. The momentum meant I pulled it over and landed face down on the grass with Anxious already prancing about on my back, enjoying the delightful new game I'd just invented.

"Um, that isn't a pole you're grabbing hold of, you know."

I turned my head and stared into the face of a very pretty young woman who looked mid-twenties. She was smiling, her heavy lipstick making her appear permanently happy, with thick eyelashes, pencil thin eyebrows, and a deep tan. She nodded down, so I looked and found I was squeezing something I wasn't meant to be and pulled my hand away sharpish.

"I'm so sorry! I was falling and just reached out. I didn't even see you."

"A likely story. Grabbing stranger's boobs is grounds for assault!"

"I swear it was an accident! Where did you even come from? It was an honest mistake. I would never—"

"It's okay. I'm just messing with you. I was coming around the corner of the tent and saw you start to go over. I rushed forward then you grabbed me. Easily done."

We both sat up and rubbed at our heads, but there was no harm done unless I'd grabbed her too hard, so asked, "Is it okay?"

"What?"

"Your, er, chesticle?" I smiled, hoping I'd lightened the mood, and wasn't digging a deeper hole for myself.

"That's the first time I've ever heard them called that, but yeah, I'm fine. I'm Clarissa, by the way."

"Max. Nice to meet you."

"And you. Although, it feels like we're already quite close, doesn't it?"

I scooted away a little, then clambered to my feet, dislodging Anxious, and reached out to help her up. "It does. Sorry again."

"No biggie. Max, don't look so freaked out. I know it was an accident."

"Okay, thank you. Are you camping or in a van?"

"We have a tent, and I work at one of the stalls. Just taking a breather. It's been manic the last hour. I didn't expect it to be so busy."

"It's definitely a day for the pie eaters," I agreed.

"And for murder."

"What do you know about it?" I asked, my heart rate increasing.

"More than the cops, that's for sure."

"Do tell," I said, smiling at my new friend.

"Why? What's your interest? Oh, you're the bloke who found the body under his van. I heard about you. Okay, so, here's the lowdown."

Chapter 17

"I used to hang with Tank."

"That surprises me."

"Why? You don't even know me."

"Because my dog likes you, and he's extremely picky about his friends."

Anxious looked up and wagged, so Clarissa flopped to the grass right there and patted her thighs. Anxious crawled up her legs cautiously, mindful of her bare skin, then nestled on her Adidas shorts, the red stripes over black looking cool. The fact her legs and the rest of her were covered in tattoos didn't bother him or me. Each to their own.

I sat beside her and she continued. "He was a fun guy, a real party animal, and for a few years I was really into it. We met doing the festival circuit and always had a great time. His brother was a bore, and always moody, and he and that wife of his were always arguing. Kelly's a good person, but super-straight and not into the party scene, but we get along well enough."

"So you knew Tank really well? How well did you know Tim?"

"Quite well. He even tried it on with me once. I told Tank and he went ape. They had a massive fight. Tank was a womaniser, but single, but he never made a pass at me as I was only just gone twenty back then."

"This is news to me. Thanks for sharing."

"Max, you don't know the half of it. Tank was a rough kind of bloke, granted, and not the most reliable, but he was a good man underneath all the booze and the constant scheming. He was a lost soul. Couldn't seem to find his way in the world. You know what I mean?"

"I do. Some spend their whole lives searching for something and never seem to find the one thing that can give them peace."

"Yeah, and I thought maybe I was the same, but one day I woke up with a hangover and that was me done. No more booze or anything harder, no messing around with trouble-makers, and I got my act together. We remained friends, but it wasn't the same. He was still the same old Tank. Lost. Looking for love, unable to conform or live how others thought he should. A bit like you, I guess. He went his own way and played by his own set of rules. I loved that about him. Anyway, we drifted apart, but kept in touch for a while. The last year or so I hardly ever saw him, as he got sacked by the others."

"I heard about that. Clarissa, what does this have to do with the deaths though? With Tank's death? I don't get it."

"I'm not sure I do exactly, but here's what I do know. Tank would never, ever ride under a vehicle. He's been here loads of times, so knows about the access, and he was into the campervan scene. Not a real vanlifer, but he spent his fair share of time living in various vans over the years as he couldn't keep a roof over his head otherwise. He knew vans is what I'm saying. He wouldn't try to sneak in under yours. No way. I mean, c'mon. Even I know that if you tried, you'd be ripped to shreds on a regular road, let alone when a low-slung VW went over those stupid speed bumps."

"So what are you saying?"

"That something else happened. Something awful. Someone put him there, or he was almost dead and crawled under to hide from someone. It's the only thing that makes sense."

"I'd considered that too. I can't figure out how he could have got under without us seeing though."

"Easy. He could have done it when it was dark. Slipped under, hid, then died. Or he was put there when you were asleep." Clarissa shrugged.

"You've given me plenty to think about, and thank you for the better understanding of those involved. One more question?"

"Shoot." Clarissa grinned, seemingly enjoying herself.

"Who do you think did it, and why?"

Clarissa laughed. "That's two questions."

"Sorry."

"No biggie. My money is on Tina. She's so uptight and utterly obsessed with the business. She resented Tim, and hated Tank. If Tank was up to no good and maybe pushing for money, she might have just decided to deal with him and her husband at the same time."

"And Nancy?"

"Who knows? Maybe she got a taste for it so offed her as well. Or maybe it was just one of those things."

"Poison is a bit of a stretch, though, isn't it? Normal people don't have access to anything that could kill someone the way they died. One minute they seemed fine, the next they were face-down in their pies. I've encountered poisoning before, and it was nothing like that."

"Have you considered the alternative?" Clarissa smiled like she knew how to do it, and I had to ask.

"What's that?"

"Maybe they weren't poisoned."

"Then how did they die? There was no blood, so what could have done it?"

"Sorry, Max, but you should have seen your face. I have no idea! It's a right mystery you've got yourself involved in, and that's for sure. Look, I better get back. We might not have won any prizes yesterday, but we're still flat out busy and it will only get worse, or better, depending on your perspective. Nice meeting you. And watch those grabby hands of yours. Not all ladies will be so forgiving of your perverted ways." With a wink and a cheeky smirk, Clarissa left.

I stared down at my hand and told it, "Behave. That could have got me into a whole heap of trouble."

Anxious whined, sad to see our new friend leave.

"I liked her too. Come on, let's get back to the pitch. Time for some sitting and to think things over. We're getting close, Anxious. I can feel it in my bones."

Back at home, and settled in my chair with a lovely brew, I studied one of the pies I'd picked up at the stall before I left. Kelly was keen for me to try them and offer my expert opinion, but I knew they would be amazing. I studied the packaging, which was simple yet ideal for takeaway. Most came without, but Kelly wanted to show off. I compared it to some of the other wrappers from the bin I'd forgotten to empty yesterday, and was about to have a cheeky nibble when the list of ingredients caught my eye.

There weren't too many, but like most food nowadays, especially anything that the makers wanted to last a while, there were always a few additives. In this case, all the pies had E508. A simple salt derivative, we used to use it as a thickener, but also as a flavour enhancer as it was basically salt. Otherwise known as potassium chloride, it was a common substance derived from either sea water or old salt deposits in lakes, and a common supplement to help with low potassium levels. Other ingredients included the usual gelatine, but thankfully the predominant ingredients were what you'd expect. Natural, healthy in moderation, although the list on some of the pies was less wholesome than I'd have expected.

Could this be the answer I was looking for? I grew excited, as it was so obvious yet so out there that for a moment I doubted even the possibility of this being the answer to at least part of the mystery. I knew one thing for certain: I had to learn more. After putting the pie back as I'd lost my appetite, I sorted through the various packaging and kept any that I thought might help prove my case, then binned the rubbish in the bin beside the path and hurried over to the food stalls. Bypassing where Min was still working, I headed to Pie in the Sky's pitch.

Jake was sweating his way through a storm of customers and I had no choice but to wait in line. Once it was my turn, I told his assistant that I wanted to have a word with Jake, so she tugged at his apron until he turned to face her, then she hitched a thumb in my direction.

He scowled at me and grunted, "You're that bloke with Kelly and Tina."

"Not really. Can I have a word? It's important. Very important."

"It'll have to be quick. We're snowed under." With a nod of his head for me to follow, he marched through a flap in the back wall of the marquee so I skirted around the customers and headed to the rear, then met him by a van where he was swigging water from a bottle.

"Sorry to drag you away from your customers. How are you holding up? We heard that the results were inconclusive, and I know this is hard but I wanted to talk to you about it."

"Max, isn't it?" I nodded. "What business is this of yours? I'm barely holding it together and I don't need you pestering me. Nancy would want me to carry on, I know she would, but it's so hard I just want to burst out crying."

"I understand, and I don't want to upset you. You probably heard that I've been involved in what's been going on. That I found a man under my van, and that Kelly and Tina don't think Tim's death was an accident."

"I heard. I'm sure you mean well, but it was an accident. I acted hysterically when she died, claiming it was murder, but it wasn't. Nancy had a scare last year, and she'd been taking things easier, but the excitement got too much for her. After Tim collapsed, it got her stressed. I told her I'd handle things, but she always wanted to be involved, the silly woman, and look what it did to her."

"You're sure it was natural causes?"

"Of course! You do what you want, but I'll play no part in it. She's gone, they're all gone. It's these damn pies!" Jake glanced down at his apron clinging tightly to his pot belly, his skinny arms shaking, his face a mask of grief, but something else too. Was it relief?

"I just need to ask you one thing. It's about what you put in your pies."

"We only use the best ingredients," he said, instantly defensive.

"I'm sure you do. Can I ask you about the additives?"

Jake frowned. "You mean the salt?"

"The potassium chloride, to be exact."

"Everyone uses that. It's a very badly kept secret. Brings out the flavour and helps thicken and preserve. What about it?"

"Who supplies it?"

"I'm not sure. I'd have to check the paperwork. One of the regular suppliers, I assume. We get bulk orders for most things. There's no other way to do it. I think a few of us use the same people. What's this about?"

"I'm not sure," I admitted. "It might be nothing, but it might be very important. Jake, I know you're grieving, but if there's a chance this was foul play don't you want to find out?"

"It was a heart attack, nothing more. My Nancy was meant to take it easy, but she was so excited about winning and wouldn't listen to me. Leave me be. I have pies to sell." With a final swig of water, Jake left me standing there and returned to his customers. I stood, rooted to the spot, while I tried to think this through a little more and wondered if I was on a wild goose chase or had cracked at least part of this case.

Now all I had to do was catch the murderer.

I must have remained there for at least five minutes, so still I was surprised to find I was breathing when I snapped out of it. There were so many things to think about

I wasn't even sure where to start, or if I had the wrong end of the stick entirely. Was this the answer to the confusing mystery, or was I grasping at straws simply to have an explanation? Even if I was right, it got me no closer to solving everything, but at least I had a starting point and something to investigate. If it was the potassium chloride, then how was it administered? I knew it was deadly in the right dose if injected in liquid form, but that would mean someone had to actually give the injection, and how did they do that without being seen?

Why take the risk? What about Tank? He died a much more unusual death, didn't he? How did this tie in with the satchel found buried? Rings and guns and belt buckles? What on earth was going on here? The more I considered poisoning by pie additive, the more confused I became. Was this wishful thinking? An explanation I was grasping as otherwise I was right back to square one? A way to convince myself I could always figure things out when the reality was that nobody had even the remotest idea what truly happened or why? I decided I needed to stop thinking about it and enjoy myself. It was why we'd come.

Anxious was looking at me funny, so I apologised for ignoring him then we headed back onto the path, the crowds now out in full force as it was lunchtime. Soon it would be the death slide competition, and more and more visitors arrived and set up beside the lake on picnic blankets loaded with food, or gratefully unpacked their lightweight chairs and settled in for the show that was sure to be fun, if very bizarre. I spied Dave across the lake, waving his hands about and pointing up at his terrifying contraption while the young helper shrugged then nodded. Probably being told what he had to do for the competition and when to stop people going up for the ride of their life. I shuddered at the thought of ever going down the thing again, and vowed that once was more than enough.

Missing Min, and wondering if she needed saving from her impromptu stint as a pie vendor, I cast a final wary, and yes, suspicious glance at Jake as he served the long line of customers, then hurried past the other stalls all of which were doing a roaring trade, until we came to High Pies, the busiest of all. Poor Anxious was close to losing his cool as he sniffed constantly, head held high to catch the pie scents. A long line of drool hung from his open mouth, his tongue darted out constantly, and he had a faraway look in his eyes.

"Maybe Min made a pie for you too," I teased, smiling at the little guy as his head shot around and his focus locked on me.

He barked a question.

"Yes, I'm certain she will have. She wouldn't leave you out, would she?"

As we approached, a red-faced Min bumped straight into me, bounced back, looked up, and grinned in a most worrying manner.

"I was just coming to find you both," she shrieked, eyes wild, hair sticking out in all directions, face covered in a sheen of sweat.

"Are you okay? What happened?"

Anxious barked loudly and began to paw at her legs so she bent and rubbed his head, still grinning, then shot upright.

"I did it! Kelly showed me what to do and after a few, er, practice pies, I finally did it. I have made the perfect pie!" she declared, beaming from ear to ear, hopping from one foot to the other, clutching a brown paper bag tight to her chest.

Anxious whined, eyes locked on the bag.

"Yes, I made you one too! In fact I made not just two perfect pies but loads. Enough for us all!"

"Careful," I warned, the smile and good mood contagious, "you're going to wear out the exclamation mark at this rate."

"I don't care! It was such fun and Kelly was a great teacher. Come on, let's go and eat them right now."

Without waiting for us to agree, she spun on her heels and raced along the path, skipping and humming to herself. Anxious and I exchanged a bemused look then hurried to catch up, the smell of pie in her wake tantalising.

By the time we got to our pitch, Min had already got plates out and was wielding a knife in a worrying manner. Her eyes were glazed, her face was sweaty, but she was beyond happy and I couldn't quite figure out why making a pie had left her so euphoric.

"Min, what's got into you? Did you have a sneaky glass of wine or something? You're so hyped. Are you okay?"

"I'm fine," she trilled, eyes never still, constantly glancing from me to Anxious to the bag of pies on the table. She swished the knife and asked, "Anyone want pie? Prepare to be blown away."

Anxious barked in the affirmative, I nodded with a confused smile, and Min continued to hop from foot to foot like she'd won the lottery. With a nod, the love of my life tore the pies from the bag, set them out like they were diamond-encrusted on the plates with the utmost care, beamed at us again, and asked, "Ready?"

"Yes, we're ready," I giggled, noting Anxious was now hopping around like Min and just as excited.

"Then prepare to be amazed!" Min cut into a pie and just like that I had an epiphany.

I knew who the killer was, and why. Now I just had to prove it.

Chapter 18

"Well?" Min frowned as she stared at me intently, eyes focused even as she wiped the sweat from her forehead and tried to tame her hair.

"Best pie I've ever eaten." I smiled and nodded, meaning it. "I don't know how you did it, but it was absolutely incredible. What did you do to make it so fantastic? It tastes so much better than the ones Kelly and Tina sell, and they were some of the best I've ever had."

"Aha, that would be telling. Kelly showed me the secret to making them really shine, but it's too involved to do in the regular ones they sell."

"Whatever it is, it worked. You should be proud of yourself."

"I know it's silly, but I am. Kelly and Tina were so kind and patient, going over everything and letting me get stuck in. Mind you, they made me work for it. You should see how many pies they sell. It's incredible."

"And was Tina coping? It's a lot to deal with after Tim dying."

"I was surprised she stayed, but the business means so much to her and she refused to let Kelly deal with it alone. I said I'd stay and help, but they insisted I should leave. I think they're excited about the pie rolling competition, and the stalls are closing for an hour to do it. They should be starting soon. Kelly said to meet them over at the death slide and that I can be the one to set their pie off from the top."

"Um, that's a great honour." I tried to remain serious as Min was clearly pleased to be chosen, but couldn't keep the smile off my face.

"Hey, no teasing. It will be fun, and we get to go first as they won the competition yesterday. Shall we clean up then head over?"

"Sure thing. There's only a few plates and that knife you kept waving around. Min, are you sure you didn't have a few sneaky drinks? You were so hyper."

"That will be the secret ingredient," she sniggered.

"Which was?"

Min mimed zipping her mouth shut then winked before laughing.

Anxious snuffled around, searching for more pie, then huffed and lay down.

I sorted out the few plates while Min freshened up, then we joined the throng of jubilant people milling around beside the lake, astounded at how many were in the water ready to catch the pies, the stewards spaced out evenly so they could act as markers for each competitor. We made it to the death slide eventually, and found Kelly and Tina beside the monstrous contraption talking to Dave, the other competitors clutching their pies like prized possessions. I spied Jake with his assistant, their heads together looking intense, most of the others in a similar state of anxiety.

Why were they taking this so seriously? It was amusing at best, and just some light fun, surely? They clearly felt otherwise, and there was a palpable tension in the air.

I caught sight of the surly detective talking with his brother and Mark, and the two young officers watching from the edge of the small group of competitors, seemingly the only ones taking any notice of those around them. I wondered how they'd fared this morning and if there was any news. It would have to wait, as Min tugged at my arm and dragged me over to Kelly and Tina.

Kelly introduced Min to Dave who nodded gruffly, distracted by the press of nervous people closing in on us, keen to get the pie rolling underway. Dave excused himself and headed over to the base of the death slide and began organising things, which mostly consisted of him snapping at the people milling about until they formed a line, clutching their pies like their lives depended on it.

"Why is everyone so serious?" I asked Kelly. "And why are you both so nervous?" I glanced at Tina who kept muttering to herself, her eyes narrowed, glaring at the others like something bad was about to happen.

Kelly nudged Tina to get her attention and Tina, distracted, and glancing at me before checking out the others again, said, "It's a big deal for everyone. Along with the giant pie competition, this is how you get your name out there. It's supposed to be harmless fun, but the local media coverage you get really boosts business, not to mention the afternoon sales you make. If you win, you sell literally hundreds more pies than you would otherwise."

"Even though you guys won yesterday? Surely that's the main event?"

"Max, this is a cutthroat business and that was yesterday. Today is all that matters now. We have to win." Tina was deadly serious and I was about to make a joke, but thought better of it when Kelly nodded solemnly.

"I don't think I should be the one to roll the pie," stammered Min, realising how much was at stake.

"You should," snapped Tina. "Sorry, that came out wrong. We want you to do it. You're our lucky charm. You've both been so kind, and we can't think how else to repay you. I'm a bag of nerves so can't do it, and I'm barely holding it together now Tim's gone."

"And I'm even more nervous," laughed Kelly. "Look at my hands." Kelly held out her hands which were shaking badly, then dropped her arms by her sides. "Please do it, Min. For us. For Tim's memory."

"Yes, do it for Tim," agreed Tina.

"If you're sure?"

"We are," said Tina, smiling, but looking like she was about to burst into tears. She handed Min the pie she'd kept in her bag and just before Min took it Anxious leaped, and everyone gasped.

I grabbed him mid-air, his mouth open, already dreaming of his prize, and Min snatched the pie from his gaping maw just in time. A sigh of relief and nervous laughs erupted as I cradled the sneaky chappy then set him down with a warning not to steal. I kissed Min for good luck, then she nodded to us before she approached the foot of the death slide, the competitors stepping aside to let her pass.

A hush fell over them as they watched her ascend, and from somewhere a loudspeaker announced that the pie rolling competition was about to begin. A loud cheer erupted from around the festival as Min climbed higher and higher. I felt ill just watching her ascend, but was thankful I didn't have to go up.

When she reached the dizzying heights of the summit, Min waved, then stood and faced the lake, the pie in her hands almost too small to see. She crouched, the crowd fell silent, then she rolled the pie and stood. Everyone applauded. Min leaned over to follow its progress, making my heart leap into my mouth, and I watched as the pie flew off the end of the slide, soaring in a high arc and almost right over to the other side of the lake.

A child was lifted up by his father and caught the pie with two hands to a huge cheer and a raucous round of applause as a steward waded over and stood beside the grinning man and boy. The marker was now set for everyone else to try and beat.

"Was that good?" I asked Kelly.

"Brilliant! We've never got it that far before and always used to win. Mind you, it's a new slide, so who knows if it's good enough."

"I think it is. That was really well done," said Tina, wiping away a tear.

Dave accompanied Min as she rushed back over to us, a huge smile on her face. "How did I do?" she asked, brimming with pride and clearly sure she'd done well.

"You did great!" beamed Kelly.

"Very well done," agreed Tina. "Thank you, Min."

"It was my pleasure."

"You showed everyone how it's meant to be done," said Dave, smiling. "That was the first pie roll down the new death slide, and very impressive. It went off without a hitch."

"Yes, the new slide has been great," said Kelly. "Everyone loves it. It was a great investment, Dave, and I know you're proud of it. The old one was here for so many years and we were sad to see it go, but this new one is brilliant. People love it."

"It took a lot of work, but it was worth it. The guys who helped me build it knew what they were doing, and it's certainly going to pay for itself with all the events lined up for this year."

"As long as nobody else dies on it," I said, almost breezily.

Everyone turned to me, shocked by my words.

"What did you just say?" asked Dave, rubbing his palms on his grubby jeans then bunching his fists.

"Max, what are you talking about?" asked Min.

"I'm sorry. I didn't get the chance to talk to you about this beforehand. I spoke to Jake earlier, and asked him about one of the ingredients in the pies, and suddenly everything made sense."

"What made sense?" asked DI Mike Almond, as he and his fellow officers appeared. "It seems you've been interfering, Max, and I warned you."

"Sorry, Max," said Jim with a sympathetic smile. "We tried to tell Mike that you're a nice guy and aren't in anyone's way, but he wouldn't listen."

"No, I wouldn't, because I heard you'd been pestering Jake and his wife's hardly even cold! You were warned to back off."

"Max is about to explain, aren't you?" said Min, coming to my defence.

"I am. Min, I wanted to tell you first, but now it's too late. It was him." I pointed at Dave. "Dave is the one you want. Watch him."

"Dave?" Tina turned to him. "What's he talking about?"

"I have no idea. You're a loon, mate. You can't go around accusing people of... What exactly are you accusing me of?"

"This has gone on long enough," hissed Mike. "Max, you need to leave."

"No, I need to let people know the truth."

"What's this about?" asked Jake as he barged past the young officers, a pie clutched tightly in his hand. "Is it about my Nancy? Do you have any news?" he asked Mike.

"Jake, it was Dave. He killed Tim and Nancy. He's also responsible for Tank's death."

"This is ridiculous!" hissed Dave, glaring at me. "Why on earth would I hurt anyone?"

"I'm sorry, Jake, and you, Tina. I wish there was another way to tell you this, but it has to happen now. Nancy and Tim were having an affair. They saw something they shouldn't have seen the night before last, the evening before the festival started. Dave knew he had to cover it up. They must have all spoken and he was worried they'd tell what happened even if it meant their own secret was known."

"You aren't making any sense, Max," said Frank. "I think you have a screw loose. Why would Dave kill them because they were having an affair?"

"My Nancy would never do that. She loved me. Tim was a bad un, everyone knows that, and was always carrying on with someone."

"He tried to have a thing with Clarissa. She's the one who made me think about this from a different perspective. Why on earth would a dead man under a campervan and two pie makers being killed have anything in common? It's the slide, meaning you, Dave. You killed them because they were having second thoughts about keeping secret what they saw late the other night."

"And what would that be?" sneered Mike.

"Tank using the slide before it was ready. Something went horribly wrong. It will be easy enough to check now we know the truth. All the marks on his body weren't from a road accident, they were from him going down the slide then skidding along the ground after he went too far. There will be paint and wood fragments in the wounds, I'm sure."

"That doesn't mean anything," stammered Dave. "Maybe he did go on the slide, but only because he was part of the crew building it. He'd been here for over a month along with the other guys."

"And you never thought to mention that?" asked Kim.

"We spoke to you multiple times," said Jim. "You said you didn't know the deceased."

"Yeah, well, I didn't want any bother. But that isn't a crime. There's no proof to any of this. It's crazy."

"No, it's the truth. Tank most likely got drunk or something and went down the slide and injured himself really badly or even died. You saw him do it, you noted Tim and Nancy together, and you made a deal with them but then thought better of it and killed them."

"Oh yeah, and how did I kill them then?"

"You were a paramedic. You told me as much. For a while, I thought you might have used potassium chloride, somehow got hold of it in liquid form. It's a perfect poison, but you probably used something else. Something from back when you were a paramedic. Why did you leave, Dave? I bet if we check it was for misconduct. Stealing medicines, I expect."

"So what?! I was sacked, but there was never any proof. I was innocent."

"We have a lot to discuss, sir," said Mark, stepping forward to confront Dave.

Dave backed off to the edge of our circle and said, "There's nothing to discuss. There's no proof of any of this. It's nonsense."

"You need to come to the station to be interviewed," said Mark. "We can clear this up there."

"Don't be dumb, Mark," sighed Mike. "This is nonsense like Dave says. Max just can't stand it that he hasn't solved this supposed crime, not that this is anything but a series of accidents, so is making things up. It's sad and very desperate."

"See?" gloated Dave, relaxing and grinning.

"Why did you bury the gun and the other things in the satchel, Dave?"

"Why would I bury a Glock? What would I hide a bunch of rings and worthless junk for? You're clutching at straws now," he laughed.

"Dave, you fell for it," I sighed, shaking my head.

"Fell for what? What's this now?"

"Nobody knew what was in the satchel apart from us and a few others," said Mike, his eyes animated for the first time.

"Someone must have told me then."

"We didn't," said Min.

"Neither did we," agreed Kelly and Tina.

"And I certainly didn't," said Jake. "But this can't be true. Not my Nancy."

"I should have divorced that man years ago," said Tina, shaking her head.

"He wasn't a bad man, Tina. Just got carried away now and then," said Kelly, putting her arm around Tina's shoulder.

"He was a liar and a cheat! But he didn't deserve to be murdered!"

"Someone must have told me. I didn't do it."

"You did, and you lied about everything," I said. "You knew what was in the bag because you buried it. It was Tank's, I assume, and you took it from him and buried it. Where's your phone? We can prove it. It will have your location on it via the tracking app. That will prove you were where the satchel was buried and it will prove you put Tank under our van." I turned to the young officers and said, "Listen, this is important. Watch him. Understand? Watch him." Jim nodded knowingly but Kim looked confused. There was no time to explain more, but I prayed this would play out as I hoped.

"It's…" Dave glanced up at the death slide and I immediately remembered seeing him give his phone to the young man earlier.

"That lad has it, doesn't he?"

"His was out of charge and we needed pictures of the competitors," stammered Dave, then he made a break for it, and barged past Jake and raced towards the death slide.

"Get him!" shouted Jake. "He murdered my Nancy."

Everyone, apart from Mike and Frank, rushed after the retreating killer, but we were no match for Anxious who tore off ahead, clearly understanding enough to know that Dave had to be stopped.

Dave shoved people aside and tore up the steps of the death slide.

"Anxious, no! It's too dangerous," I shouted in a panic, but he was focused on his prey and couldn't hear me above everyone complaining about Dave.

He paused only briefly at the bottom of the steps before deciding he could manage them and bounded after Dave, barking in warning as he sped upwards.

Chapter 19

Only one person at a time was allowed to go up the death slide during the competition so nobody tried to put the others off, and luckily the latest contestant had just descended before Dave shoved them aside, so I didn't have to worry about that. What I did have to worry about was Anxious. My own fears forgotten, I took the steps three at a time, my long legs helping me power up the terrible contraption and hopefully catch up with Anxious before he got hurt or worse.

Turn after turn, up and up we climbed, Dave and the little guy always out of reach. Anxious barked incessantly, warning his quarry to stop or he'd get a serious ankle biting, but Dave wasn't about to risk the police getting his phone and would stop for nothing, not even the risk of a good gnaw by the fearless Jack Russell.

The incessant barking grew more insistent, so I assumed Dave was flagging and Anxious was getting closer, so I redoubled my efforts, pleased with my fitness levels, but still tiring. I rounded a corner and gasped as I looked out at the sea of people in the water and lining the lake. We were really high now, only one flight of stairs to go. I barrelled ahead, focusing on the steps, then reached the platform where the young man was pinned to the railing. Dave grabbed his phone off the lad just as Anxious reached him.

"Here, boy. Good job," I gasped, slapping my thighs to encourage Anxious to move away from the edge.

Anxious yipped, spun from Dave, and trotted over, breathing heavily.

"You can't prove anything now."

"I can just take the phone off you," I reminded him.

"Won't do you any good if it gets ruined in the water, will it?" crowed Dave, grinning as he snatched a sack from the pile, backed up to the bar across the slide, then grabbed hold with one hand and swung himself out.

"No!" I shouted, and ran forward. "Grab the phone," I shouted to the young man, but he stared at me blankly, utterly confused.

Anxious darted between my legs, believing I was talking to him, and then he was gone. I ran forward and watched Dave whizz down the death slide, Anxious right behind him. With no time to lose, I took a sack and launched myself down the death-defying almost vertical drop, my heart in my mouth, all my fears coming to the fore at once as I sailed through the air before bumping back onto the solid slide with a relieved grunt only to feel my stomach flip as I pelted towards the lake at unimaginable speed.

The world whizzed by in a blur of fear and stress about Anxious and my own relatively short future if anything went awry. Knowing I had to, I opened my eyes and watched Dave reach the end of the slide and shoot out into the water, bewildered people clearing the area before he smashed a few heads.

Anxious was right behind him and I was coming up on him fast, my size meaning I'd descended faster than either of them. With my fingers crossed, I hit the end of the slide a moment after Anxious and yet because he was so light, he would travel much further than me or Dave. As I soared, I tried to streamline myself as much as I could and managed a somersault so I was facing forward, arms outstretched, trying to reach Anxious before he got hurt.

Dave landed with an almighty splash just as Anxious sailed past. Was this all for nothing? Then Anxious chomped down with a fast snatch of his head and grabbed the phone between his teeth, jaws locked tight on the prize. I wasn't going to reach him in time, and he would hit the water fast and hard, but as I angled down I saw a sight I would never forget. There in the water, arms outstretched, looking like a goddess, was Min.

Anxious landed in her arms like she was catching a ball, and as our eyes met she smiled at me, more beautiful than ever. Utterly oblivious to my own impending crash landing, I hit the water with a spectacular belly flop that took the wind out of me and then I went under.

Surfacing with a splutter and a very sore stomach, I saw Min wade through the shallows to a loud round of applause, everyone speculating as to why a Jack Russell instead of a pie had gone down the slide along with two men who should have known better than to interrupt the competition. I kept my head down as people on the bank snapped photos, and hurried towards Dave who was already at the shoreline. He glanced back in a panic when he saw me, then smiled, thinking he'd got away, and turned his attention to Min and Anxious, the phone dry and still in his mouth.

I splashed through the water and got onto land just as Dave reached Min who was unaware of his presence until Anxious barked a garbled warning, still holding the phone.

The announcer said something over the tannoy system, then a perturbed woman shouted something out from the top of the death slide and I turned in time to see her squat, then release her pie down the slide. Seemingly, nothing was going to stop the competition from continuing, and to be fair, most people had no idea what was going on beyond that two men and one dog had decided to interrupt proceedings to have a go on the slide.

Everything seemed to move in slow motion as time almost froze. As I staggered through the silty water at the shore, Dave reached out to grab his phone from Anxious' mouth. I shouted, "No!" and stumbled forward as a rush of air passed by my left ear like a bullet from a gun. I ducked, instinct taking over, fearing someone was shooting at us, and crashed onto my hands and knees on the short grass.

My head shot up in time to see the pie smash into the back of Dave's head. Whatever was in the crust must have been against competition rules, as the pie still looked perfect as Dave crashed to the ground at Min's feet and the golden pie landed with a faint thud on the murderous madman's back.

Anxious dropped the phone into Min's hand as he wriggled free of her grasp, landed on Dave's head, then hopped over and snatched the pie with his bared teeth. He sat on Dave's back and merrily tucked in to the pastry encrusted cheese and potato treat. A man in a green high-vis jacket waded past me and hurried over then stood next to them and raised his matching flag. The spectators cheered and the woman atop the death slide whooped for joy. So far she was in the lead and there was now no evidence she'd cheated and used something other than the listed ingredients to make her pie fly further than everyone else's.

With adrenaline pumping, but the fear and stress fading now I knew Anxious was okay, I stood and hurried over to them where Kim and Jim were hauling Dave to his feet. With a smirk, Kim read him his rights while Jim clicked the cuffs tight around his wrists pulled behind his back.

I smiled at Min then bent and patted Anxious who was sitting with his head cocked, licking his lips. "Great job, buddy, but you had me worried there for a moment. You saved the day, though, and caught the killer, so you deserved your treat."

"Hey, don't forget about me," said Min. "Did you see the catch I made? How cool was that?"

"Very," I agreed, reaching out and hugging her tight, my legs suddenly like jelly. "Are you alright?"

"Me? I'm fine. It's you and Anxious I'm worried about, although I think he's recovered just fine! Max, that was crazy. What were you thinking?"

"That I had to save Anxious and stop Dave destroying his phone."

"I'll take that," growled DI Mike Almond as he appeared with the rest of the group, everyone out of breath and staring at us in astonishment.

"I don't think so, Mike." Mark snatched the phone from the man's thick fingers and stepped back out of his reach.

"What are you playing at, Mark?" hissed Mike. "I'm the lead on this case, and that's evidence."

"I know, and I'm going to ensure nothing happens to it. You need to retire, Mike, just like we all do. We're jaded, tired, and you," he jabbed a finger at Frank, "need to stop protecting your brother. You're as bad as him. Neither of you would listen to these nice people, or our two new recruits, and you would have blown this if it wasn't for Max. It's embarrassing. You should both be ashamed. I know I am. Two people dead, most likely by poisoning, one seemingly dead because of that death slide, a bag of evidence, and you still couldn't be bothered to give it more than a passing thought."

Mike and Frank opened and closed their mouths but no words came, and they barged through the small crowd that had gathered, leaving us astonished.

"I never thought I'd see the day when DI Mike Almond let himself be insulted and just took it," said Jim, watching them go.

"It's about time I stood up to him and his brother. Time for me to retire. I'm sorry this wasn't handled properly." Mark turned to Tina and Jake. "You have my sincerest apologies. I knew something wasn't right, but didn't push Mike hard enough or just go over his head and get this mess sorted out sooner. I'm sorry for your loss."

"We understand," said Tina. "I still can't believe this is true."

"Or me," said Jake. He focused on Dave and asked, "Why would you kill them? Were they really having an affair?"

"You're so dumb, both of you. Your beloved partners were carrying on with each other right under your noses and you had no idea. That idiot, Tank, had been working for me for a while. He was always good for a laugh, but boy was he thick. We were finalising the death slide and had to get it into position, last-minute rush as usual, but he got wasted. He was so drunk he thought it would be a good idea to climb up and test it out, but it wasn't set up correctly and I had to chase him up there the other night and stop him."

"But you didn't, did you?" I asked

"No, I didn't. He was almost comatose, he was so drunk, and slipped and went down the slide, but it pointed over to the side road and he flew off the end and landed badly on the gravel and slid across. I ran to help but he was almost gone, and then I spied Tim and Nancy in the trees. They were obviously up to no good. The fact they were half undressed gave the game away." Dave leered and chuckled, and I had to stop Jake from punching him.

"You threatened to tell if they reported what happened?" Jake asked.

"Sure. What else could I do? They promised they'd keep quiet if I didn't tell on them and they agreed to help hide Tank. We just dragged him under the nearest van, which I guess was yours," he told me. "He was dead by then, and I figured it would look like he got stuck under your VW when you drove in."

"But you couldn't leave it at that?" I asked.

"Nancy and Tim came to see me early the next morning in a panic, and I knew they would tell. But you lot and your pies are so obsessed that they said they'd wait until the competition was over, so I took my chance and did what I had to do." Dave shrugged. He genuinely didn't seem to care that he'd committed murder.

"Why bury the bag? What were the things in it for?"

"No idea. Tank was always up to no good, so I guess it was just a few of his things. I burned his wallet but didn't know what to do with the rest, so buried it. Figured I'd deal with it once the festival was over. So stupid."

"How did you kill them?" asked Min.

Everyone held their breath, waiting for an answer, but Dave chuckled, his lip curled in a sneer, and said, "No chance. I've said more than enough. Don't suppose it matters what with you having my phone."

"I think he's missing the point here, Max," said Jim, laughing right back at Dave.

"I think you're right. So you worked it out? What I said?"

"Watch out for him, is what you said. I noticed it straight away."

I smiled at the smart officer, certain he'd go far.

"Ah, so it wasn't about the phone at all?" asked Kim, nodding her understanding.

"Not really. Sure, it will be easier to get the data, but it's the watch that's important."

Jim turned Dave around and unfastened his smart watch, then held it up for everyone to see.

"Dave told me he's into running and always likes to get his step count in every day. He has it set up to track his routes so he can see the distances and the time it takes. It basically records his every movement. That's an expensive piece of kit. It's linked to the app on his phone, but as long as we have the watch I'm sure the tech people can get the data. But now we have both, so there's no denying where he was or what he did."

"And it's waterproof," said Jim, nodding.

"It doesn't mean anything," protested Dave. "All it does is prove I had a late night walk. Maybe I hid Tank's body, but there's no proof I killed Nancy or Tim."

"No?" I asked, confronting him. "I would imagine a thorough search of your van will bring up all kinds of interesting things you stole when you were a paramedic. I bet you've got quite a store of medications and things that could have killed them. Once that's been checked, they can test Nancy and Tim and see what you used. It's over, Dave. You killed them and admitted it. You're done."

"They would have ruined me! All the work I put in and that idiot Tank would have destroyed everything. Nancy and Tim had to go. I couldn't let them tell. I just couldn't."

Kim and Jim led Dave away, leaving us rather shell-shocked, and some of us much wetter than we'd have liked. I shivered despite the sunshine, as there was no happy ending for those left behind, just a sadness and now the harsh reality that their spouses had cheated the night before they died.

"Thank you, Max," murmured Jake. "You figured it out and I truly appreciate that."

"Me too," mumbled Tina, clearly still in shock. "How did you do it? Why did you think it was Dave?"

"When I met that woman, Clarissa, she'd said Tank was a handful, and a womaniser, but I'm afraid to say that she said the same thing about Tim. That got me to thinking about things. Then I wondered if they'd been poisoned, but that didn't explain Tank's death. It didn't add up. He couldn't have been dragged under Vee. We would have known. He had to have sustained his injuries here, and what's the most terrifying, dangerous thing around? The death slide, of course."

"But that still doesn't explain why you assumed it was Dave," said Min. "And I'm still annoyed about you not telling me."

"I'm sorry, there just wasn't time. I wanted to, but it happened so fast."

"So what made you certain?" asked Min.

"Getting Dave to admit what was in the bag when he shouldn't have known. That was a dumb mistake on his part."

"Yes, but why suspect him?" Min pushed.

"Have you seen that thing?" I turned to the death slide and shuddered. "Only a madman would build such a contraption."

Anxious yowled in agreement and shuddered, too, his high-pitched wail ringing out around the site, causing all the other dogs to return his call with a bark or whine of their own.

Min squeezed my hand and told me, "You never have to go down another death slide again."

"Good, because I don't think I could handle it. What I would like is another one of your pies."

Min's eyes lit up and she whispered, "I might have hidden a couple more as a treat. But there were only two left."

Anxious' ears perked up and he sat obediently, tail swishing across the grass.

"Looks like we're sharing," I laughed.

Chapter 20

Min yawned, then stretched her arms overhead as she stepped down from Vee and smiled at me. "Morning," she sighed.

"Good morning. Sleep well?"

"Like a log. After the last few days, all the questions, the police back and forth, consoling Tina and helping Kelly, I was beat last night."

"Me too. But at least everything got sorted in the end. I feel sorry for Tina and Jake as it's a shame Dave changed his story and is now denying everything, but it doesn't make much difference."

"Not now they found those stolen meds in his van. Some of them were really dangerous. He must have been at it for years."

"That's what Kim and Jim said. And they have his route tracked and it shows he was exactly where he shouldn't have been. He did it, we heard him admit it, and I bet he changes his mind and accepts a deal by pleading guilty."

"They won't give him a deal, will they?"

"Maybe. I don't mean let him off, but they might reduce his sentence. I can't see him getting out for a very long time though."

"Who knew pies could be so deadly?"

Anxious's ears twitched at the mention of pies, but then he resumed his napping once he realised it was a false alarm.

"At least it's over now. I can't believe they even continued the pie rolling competition on Saturday."

"Only because nobody knew what on earth was happening apart from us. It's a shame Kelly and Tina didn't win, but they were happy enough with how they did. To be frank, I don't think Tina was even that upset once she calmed down."

"About the pies?"

"No, about her husband being murdered. They obviously didn't have a very good relationship."

"It happens. She was upset, but coped, and was even better yesterday when they were packing up. We have the place pretty much to ourselves today. Anxious and I have already been for a walk, and it's really quiet. No day visitors, no stalls, just a few people in vans and a couple of people camping. We have to leave today, but most went yesterday because there were no more competitions."

"And it was a perfect evening. Just us, no police, no questions to answer. It was sweet of Kim and Jim to come and fill us in on everything that happened, and I'm amazed the three old duffers actually retired. That was a surprise."

"I think Mark's admission that it was time they left the force, especially Mike and Frank, hit home. It's for the best."

"And look at you, my hero. You did it again. I can't believe you didn't tell me."

"I know, but like I said, it happened too fast. I had my suspicions, but then I did suspect a lot of people, and it was only confirmed when Dave knew what was in the bag."

"I wish we knew why those things were there."

"Sometimes you don't get all the answers. It doesn't matter. The main thing is Dave's where he belongs. Let me show you something."

"Another mystery?" Min giggled, her eyes questioning.

"The biggest," I said with a smile. I stood, then approached, and walked Min around to the driver's side of my beloved campervan.

"More graffiti? What does it say?"

"I still can't work it out. They've added to it, but it makes no sense. Is that a v? Does that look like an r to you, or is it abstract? Again, the colours are nice, and it matches Vee's orange and white two-tone, but I don't get it."

"Maybe it's different people? You know you're quite famous online now, with people discussing your exploits in forums, and even posting videos on YouTube. Lots of vanlifers here knew who you were, and will have read about the artwork on the van. I bet people are falling over themselves to add to it and boast to their virtual friends."

"Maybe, but do you think we should be worried? What if it's a stalker?"

"Max, relax. It's just a group of people having fun at our expense. And bedsides, I like it. I can't wait to see what the finished artwork looks like. You won't paint over it, will you?"

"I don't think so. It's only on the lower panels, and it does look funky. Gives it a retro, sixties, hip vibe."

"Exactly. It matches your long hair and chilled look. Now, I have to use the bathroom. I'm bursting. Is coffee on?"

"It sure is. I'll pour you a cup the moment you return."

Min kissed my cheek then skipped off, her body radiating energy and happiness.

Although it hadn't been the trip I'd expected, the Sunday had begun chaotically but gradually calmed once we'd dealt with the authorities and Kelly and Tina, and we'd had a lovely evening just the three of us once the site had cleared and silence finally descended. Times like those were special, and didn't happen often enough. Maybe soon it would be like that every day. I truly hoped so.

Just a few months to go and it would be the year deadline for the decision to be made, and I both anticipated and dreaded it in equal measure. Everything was going so well, but was it going well enough? Did Min trust that I had changed for good and would never return to my old ways? I think she did. I knew in my heart I was different now, and felt so good for upending my life and finally doing what was right. All it needed for it to be perfect was for her to be with me and Anxious. What a team we made.

I smiled at the little guy snoring, still amazed at what he'd done, and chuckled as I recalled yet again seeing him sailing through the air, tongue out, ears flapping, and snatching the phone from Dave's hand before Min caught him. But it was also a warning that none of us were indestructible. He could have been badly hurt, or worse, and I couldn't imagine life without him. I vowed to do all in my power to keep him and Min safe, and truly appreciate every moment we had together.

Min returned soon enough, and we sat and drank coffee, chatting about this and that, avoiding sensitive topics, skirting around potential plans for the future and enjoying the sunshine.

After a light lunch, no pies involved, Min packed her few things and we drove her to the station then waved goodbye as the train departed before returning to the festival so I could pack up the gazebo and sort out the kitchen. I had a few hours before the site closed, so made the most of it and once I was ready to go I sat in my chair and stared out at the lake and the looming death slide.

Anxious followed my gaze from where he was snuggled up in my lap, and whined.

"Don't worry, no more slides for us," I assured him.

With a grunt, he tucked his nose between his legs and drifted off to sleep.

I stretched out and heard a crumple from my cut-off shirt pocket, an old chequered shirt I was using for a little extra early morning warmth that Min had given me earlier and I'd forgotten I was wearing. Reaching into the pocket, I pulled out a slip of folded paper and flattened it with my palm.

"Shell Island," I read. Frowning, I turned it over, but there was nothing on the other side. I pulled out my phone and called Min, but she denied having put it there and promised me she knew nothing about it.

"What are you going to do?" she asked, voice full of concern.

"There's only one thing I can do, isn't there?"

"Max, you shouldn't go. And haven't you been there before?"

"No, I stayed at Harlech, which is really close, but never actually pitched there. It's not a proper island, just gets cut off by the tide for an hour or two some days. It's the largest campsite in the UK, maybe Europe, and meant to be amazing, so why not?"

"Because someone wants you to go there and that will absolutely mean trouble."

"Or, you're teasing and it was you."

"I swear it wasn't. Max, be careful and let me know the minute you arrive. Now I'm going to worry."

"There's no need. We'll be fine. And besides, I have my terrifying little companion to protect me."

"I bet he's curled up in your lap and snoring," she giggled.

"Yes, but when he's needed, he springs into action."

"Watch out for anything suspicious, and stay safe, Max."

"I will. See you soon. Love you."

"Love you too," Min said without pause, and that was the most perfect ending I could have ever asked for to my latest murder mystery adventure.

The End

But not really. Read on for a delicious recipe. Can you guess what it is? I know, but what else could we eat? Maybe Min even shared the secret she learned from Kelly with Max, so we can make a pie to be truly proud of.

After the recipe, there will be a few words from me about what to expect next, and don't forget, there are only two books left now, so be sure to keep reading.

Recipe

Min's Cheese and Potato Pie of Awesomeness (according to her)

Oh pie, how we love you so. Hearty, warming, perfect on a scorching summer's day or in the depths of winter when the steaming golden pastry and insanely hot filling warm your belly and delight the taste buds, a pie is also ideal as a cold snack. They're great for lunch, dinner, or any time you want to sit on the step of your campervan and watch people passing you by, feeling smug and maybe with a fresh brew too.

It's all too easy to dismiss what seems like a relatively mundane food choice, but if you can master pie making it opens up a whole other world of meal choices to add to your repertoire. You can experiment with all manner of fillings, from rich beef stew mix, any number of fillings based around leftovers, go spicy, even curried options, delicious jerk chicken, or creamy veg mixes using whatever you have to hand. But for this recipe we owe it to Max, and more especially to Min, to stick with a classic cheese and potato filling.

A shout out should go to Nigella, as this is based on one of the original Domestic Goddess' recipes. She did teach Min almost all she knows about faffing about in the kitchen.

And no matter what I do, this involves multiple pans and is not van friendly to make at all! It is, however, perfect for eating on the go. Ideal van picnic food for sure.

Let's get started.

Ingredients

For the Pastry

- Plain flour – 250g / 8oz
- Unsalted butter – 125g / 4oz - diced
- Egg – 1
- Salt – 1tsp
- Cold Water - 2tbsp

For the Filling

- Waxy potatoes – 500g / 1lb – peeled and diced
- Spring onions (scallions) – 125g / 4oz
- Mature cheddar – 150g / 5oz – half grated, half diced
- Shropshire blue – 50g / 2oz – grated
- English mustard – 1tsp
- Sour cream – 3tbsp
- Black pepper

Method

You can mix up the cheese to suit your own taste of course, but you do want something a little bit punchy! Individual flan tins, or 4-bun Yorkshire pudding trays are needed to make these. You'll have enough for 8 fab little pies.

- Firstly make the pastry. Make sure all the ingredients are cold. You can use the traditional rubbing in method or do as Min does at home. Add the flour, butter, and salt to a food processor and blitz until it resembles fine breadcrumbs. Then add the egg and ice cold water

slowly and pulse until it comes together into a ball. Wrap in clingfilm and chill for at least half an hour.
• Preheat the oven to 200C/400F.
• Now onto the filling. Boil the diced potatoes for 5-10 mins. You want them to hold their shape but be cooked through. No-one wants an *al dente* potato. Drain and let them cool a little.
• Mix the spring onions, cheeses, potatoes, and a good grinding of black pepper, followed by the mustard and sour cream to bind it all together.
• Halve the pastry, roll out and cut each half into 8 circles big enough to fill the bun trays. Fill each with an eighth of the cheesy potato filling and top with a pastry lid. Crimp the edges to seal and make a small hole for the steam to escape.
• Cook for 20 minutes. They will be pale but firm and very, very cheesy. Try to leave them to stand for 5 minutes or so to allow for easier removal from their trays.

These make a lovely lunch with a ripe tomato salad. Some even enjoy them with a dollop of ketchup, just don't tell Max.

From the Author

I hope the pie works out well. Post a picture on Facebook if it did, or even if it didn't! As we near the end of Max's case files, I already have ideas for what comes next. It's too early to share, but I'm growing more excited by the day about the next series, so stay tuned and sign up to at least one form of notification you see below. For now, let's focus on book 14, the penultimate of the series. Max is heading off to Shell Island on the North-West coast of Wales, so let's go check what he's up to in Campfires and Dead Liars. It's going to be awesome!

Be sure to stay updated about new releases and fan sales. You'll hear about them first. No spam, just book updates at www.authortylerrhodes.com.

You can also follow me on Amazon www.amazon.com/stores/author/B0BN6T2VQ5.

Connect with me on Facebook www.facebook.com/authortylerrhodes/